Élmer Mendoza

SILVER BULLETS

Translated from the Spanish by
Mark Fried

MACLEHOSE PRESS
QUERCUS · LONDON

First published in the Spanish language as *Balas de Plata*
by Tusquets Editores, Barcelona, in 2008
First published in Great Britain in 2015 by

MacLehose Press
An imprint of Quercus Publishing Ltd
Carmelite House
50 Victoria Embankment
London EC4Y 0DZ

An Hachette UK company

Esta publicación fue realizada con el estímulo del Programa de Apoyo a la Traducción
(PROTRAD) dependiente de instituciones culturales mexicanas.

This publication is supported by the Programa de Apoyo a la Traducción
(PROTRAD), an initiative of the Mexican cultural institutions.

A CIP catalogue record for this book is available
from the British Library

ISBN (HB) 978 0 85705 258 2
ISBN (TPB) 978 0 85705 259 9
ISBN (Ebook) 978 1 78206 489 3

2 4 6 8 10 9 7 5 3 1

Designed and typeset by Libanus Press in Minion
Printed and bound in Great Britain by Clays Ltd, St Ives plc

For Leonor

TRANSLATOR'S NOTE

This novel takes place in a prosperous and sweltering Mexican city of just under a million people, half an hour's drive from the Pacific and nine hundred kilometres south of the U.S. border. Culiacán, the Sinaloa state capital, lies far off the tourist track, surrounded by desert and lush, irrigated fields. Its elite still thrives on commercial agriculture, but in recent decades the trafficking of marijuana, cocaine and heroin has far outdistanced the sale of cucumbers and chilli peppers. By 2006, when the story takes place, Culiacán had become one of the country's more violent cities, its political and economic landscape transformed by the huge fortunes made and lost under hails of bullets.

The world is a dangerous place, not because of the people who are evil, but because of the people who don't do anything about it.

ALBERT EINSTEIN

The real Mexico horrifies many people, not the fact that it exists but the fact that it gets talked about.

JOAQUÍN LÓPEZ-DÓRIGA

One

Waiting room. You can tell how modern a city is, the detective thought, by the weapons you hear going off in its streets, surprised by his own unexpected conclusion, what did he know about modernism, or postmodernism for that matter, or intangible cultural heritage? Nothing. I'm just a little deer that lives in the woods. Seeing the therapist always made him nervous, so he killed time thinking about everything except the one thing he should be trying to figure out. How do they kill people in Paris, Berlin, Fiji? A door, sloppily painted ochre-yellow, swung open and a young woman emerged, her hair a mess and her face a mask of powdered eggshell. Without a glance his way, she headed straight for the stairs.

In he went. The office stank of tobacco, so much so it made you want to quit. After checking his little notebook, the therapist went right to the nub: I'm floored by the way you suppressed your instinct for self-preservation, how is it possible you didn't even kick and scream? Well, could you have said no? not me; I was a child, I couldn't run away or yell, I just couldn't; do you really believe a nine-year-old snot-nose is capable of defending himself when he's scared stiff? not me; I lost my courage, I was paralysed, I was a puppet; you can insist all you like, but I can't cope with having been abused; it goes round and round in my head and no, I am not going to just accept it as if I'd been given a pat on the back.

It was the breaking point and for nearly two years he kept running up against it, even though he prattled on about the smells,

11

the sounds, the half-light. I hate Pedro Infante's music. That you hadn't told me, Dr Parra lit another cigarette, did he like it? He didn't listen to anything else and he went to his movies too; he talked about them like they were the last beer left in the stadium; a couple of times, before it happened, he took me to the movies; I had a good time, now that memory hurts. Did he buy you popcorn? No, or in any case I forget, do I have to remember that too? is it part of the degenerative contract you told me about that other time? Not necessarily, popcorn forms part of our permanent memory, it's usually innocuous; however, in this case, given its origins, it could be an active element in your bag of poison, that toxic space where we keep all the things that alienate us as individuals from our personal history.

The detective rested his eyes on the bookcase to his right. Do you remember why I became a policeman? More or less. Well, every day I'm less sure. Then refresh my memory. When I was a little kid I wanted to be a priest, he made a long pause, Parra wrote in his notebook, Enrique wanted to be a fireman, a pilot, a frogman, all those things boys like; not me, my dream was to be a missionary in Africa or something like that, pause, and look where I ended up. You're not doing so badly. Not so well either and I don't believe, as you say, that I joined the police to protect the weak and help justice to triumph; I wanted to make easy money and get out of here as fast as I could. Yet you stayed. People get used to anything. And you made enemies of the people who could have made you rich quick. So what do you want, life's a lottery.

Office downtown. Parra in his worn-out easy chair, Edgar Mendieta in the straight-backed one he preferred to the mysterious nudity of the couch. It was a gloomy place that smelled of cheap detergent. On one of his visits he mentioned as much, but it made no difference to the doctor, who just commented that this was the cheerless part of a dissolute city. Parra looked at his watch. Edgar, you have to leave all that behind, you aren't seriously damaged and the years have brought you a lot of good, grab hold of those things; I know you think happiness is a sign of stupidity, but even if you don't believe it letting this go is one of the very few things you can still do to find some relief; and stop drinking, when you mix that with the tranquillisers the least that'll happen is you'll fall asleep in your soup; you're a success, enjoy it, and pick up your love life, you know how that puts a smile on your face, do you remember when you were going with that girl? do something, I want to see that sparkle in your eyes, that feeling that the world is your oyster; come on, look at your future another way and, oh, time's up. Parra wore a beard and he looked dirty and tired. You've never talked so much, doctor. It's because I see that you're better, a little on edge, but on balance pretty well. And because you need to get home early. Well, sure, what do you want, as a family man I try to be there for the ten o'clock news; let's leave the next appointment open, maybe you won't need it. I wish.

He went out. Distracted, he gazed up at the cloudy sky. A Lobo pickup and two black Hummers roared by pushing the other drivers aside. Their stereos were blasting out corridos and from one of them an arm tossed a beer bottle that shattered at the detective's feet. The great achievement of powerful countries is order, he muttered. Here we're worth shit. He got into his Jetta, the radio came on. "It's time for the second edition of 'Eyes on the Night,'" an announcer said, "the top radio show in town." He switched it off, nosed out into the traffic on Obregón Avenue, heavy for the hour, and drove home in silence.

He ate no supper so he would not have nightmares.

Two

It was drizzling. Was she afraid? No. Did this March rain mean anything? I do not think so. It might have brought that Brazilian song to mind or some faraway, uncaring city, but she was not up to it. Paola Rodríguez went through the gate and walked slowly towards the house: white, one storey, wooden door. When she parked across the street, she had failed to notice the S.U.V. with tinted windows a few yards in front of her, whose rain-soaked windshield hid the driver completely. Indecisive? Not a chance. Though she felt the scars of certain kisses, she moved with a determination that matched her beauty. She was glad she was getting wet, especially now that she only had Edvard Munch in her head ("The Scream") and Frida Kahlo ("The Two Fridas"). Diego was a bastard, forget him. Her mind was throbbing and she had no interest in reining it in, her red hair was mussed from the humidity and the hour. Flowers in the garden: a few roses, fewer calendulas, a bougainvillea, all barely visible in the inky darkness. A yellowish sedan in the open garage reflected the light of a bare bulb hanging from the wall. She opened the blue door with her key. American-style house with two toilets, the neighbourhood was middle class. In the street somebody's pickup headed off slowly, another neighbour started his. The squeak of the door closing should have reminded her of something, but it did not. From her bag she pulled out a black semi-automatic. It was about six in the morning and soon Bruno Canizales would get up to run, that despicable turncoat, that "I couldn't care less, I don't give a fuck about anything, sweet fuck all, less than sweet fuck all, whatever". Whew, she breathed out. She wanted him to hear her, to see her come in, to get all startled, she wanted his eyes to grow wide when he saw her Beretta dark and threatening: Paola, my love, my queen, put that down, you look terrific, but better put that away, it's so early and . . . You swine, you know perfectly well what I'm here for. She had warned him: If you leave me I'll kill you. It especially hurt that he had dumped her for that sinister dancing guy, damn the day that she introduced them. Here, meet a great friend of mine and the best dancer in the world, a true artist. Pao, don't exaggerate, please, look at how I'm blushing. All those girls frolicking around you never mattered, they're women and I understand them, even that she-devil we ran into once. He's different, and that hurts. She did not notice the living room or the kitchen, both impeccably clean. She ignored the potted plants she had brought him and the paintings that on several occasions were the subject of animated discussions.

You said you're one of those who will never marry, and me pretending to be very modern, I answered: Me too, we smiled and then it all happened.

She paused to chamber a round, then continued down the hall. Skylight. The open door of the study did not attract her attention. Nor the closed door of the guest room. At the back, the bedroom of Attorney Bruno Canizales, the love of her life, the only man a decent woman has the right to kill without remorse. She approached the door with its blessed Easter palm leaf. Silence. She opened it carefully. Your time is up, asshole. Darkness. Aggressive fragrance. She felt suddenly apprehensive, she did not like the posture of the body on the untidy bed, on top of the sheets, crosswise. You damn liar, are you sleeping off a night of wild sex? Training the pistol on him, she went up to the lamp, but did not switch it on. No need. She could see Bruno was dead.

She sat on the floor with the pistol between her legs and began to cry. I would have married you just so we could be together; angelface, I would have promised to love you and respect you until death do us part, in sickness and in health, in . . . and in adversity. I decided not to be a dummy and listen to me now. God, you can fake anything in the world except love. Beside her, his shoes. She scratched her itchy left hand with the barrel of the Beretta. Money must be coming my way, she murmured, then she put on the safety, dropped the weapon into her bag, and stood up. She contemplated the cadaver in street clothes lying on top of the unmade sheets, the pale clean-shaven face. On the chest of drawers she saw a book of hers and a card: "Pick up Dr Ripalda, 7.15. Aeroméxico." Paola Rodríguez looked at her watch: 6.08. Bruno dear, someone hated you more than I did. She left without giving a thought to the body.

Beautiful: impossible to describe her.

It was drizzling.

Three

Edgar "Lefty" Mendieta took his pistol out of the glove compartment, got out of the Jetta, stuck the gun in his belt, and left the door open. He had been listening to Herman's Hermits "There's a Kind of a Hush" on a C.D. of oldies and he could not get the tune out of his head. I hope it's one of those impossible cases, they're the ones we're best at, he thought, we never solve them and nobody cares or asks questions at three in the morning. He was wearing a black T-shirt and black jeans and a thin windbreaker the same colour. Beside an abandoned truck on the outskirts of the city, in a big lot for truckers in a place known as Piggyback, lay the body of a man not yet identified. For comfort, he put the Beretta in the pocket of his jacket while he dealt with Daniel Quiroz, crime beat reporter for "Eyes on the Night," who thanks to his connections was the first to arrive at the scene.

Lefty, do you know anything I don't know? Well, by the blue of his eyes I'd say he was Steve McQueen, an American, motorcyclist by trade. But you haven't seen him. I'm psychic, don't you remember? My man Lefty, I am whatever I may be, but I am not ungrateful, and never would I be disloyal to a buddy like you who has done me so many favours. Boss. Calling to him was Zelda Toledo, his partner, who until recently was a traffic cop and now since Sánchez retired was always at his side. Oh baby, Quiroz sighed, do you ever look good, you don't have your irons in that fire, do you Lefty? God help me, I would never get involved with a woman whose feet stink.

Oh, I would, and I'd get off sucking on her little pinkies.

The technicians had sealed the area with yellow tape and two assistants of Dr Montaño, the forensic, were doing their thing without much enthusiasm. A dust devil in the distance made plain that if February is wild, March is wilder still.

The blanket was brown and blood-soaked, emblazoned with a stag between two peaks, on it lay the body of a man, forty-five or fifty years old, the detective calculated, a metre eighty, Versace shirt, barefoot, castrated, and with a bullet in his heart. One of the officers scouring the place returned with an ostrich-leather cowboy boot, Mendieta made a face. Let's hand the case over to Narcotics, he ordered his partner, several cell phones rang out, we don't need his name to know his line of work. Not only did they castrate him, Zelda said, they also cut out his tongue, we haven't found the casings, which makes you think they killed him someplace else and brought him here. It makes no difference, any case that involves the narcos has already been solved, call Pineda so he can get in touch with Ortega, who'll be here before long anyway, and we'll see each other at the office. What should I tell the district attorney's people? she pointed at a young woman who was taking in the scene, her eyes out of orbit. Whatever you can dream up, he walked over to the white Jetta parked beyond a row of big trucks. Several drivers were nosing about, drinking coffee and eating shredded-beef tacos and beans. Two of them had seen a black Lobo dump the blanket-wrapped body, but they were not crazy enough to say so. With the Mexican police, the further away the better, same story with the killers.

*

Seventh Cavalry song. Mendieta, the detective muttered, answering a call from Briseño, his boss. Where are you? Looking at a tomato field and an army of Oaxacans picking red and green peppers, and since you called let me report that Narcotics turned up and wants rights over the gangsta-wrap, let's hand it over so we don't have problems, you know how touchy they can be. Who was it? Pineda, Señor Jealous-of-his-Turf. Let them have it and take charge of a case in Guadalupe, half an hour ago a body was reported, name Bruno Canizales, a lawyer, nominee for professional of the year, and a member of the U.S.B. The what? The Universal Small Brotherhood. Sounds like the Undercover Surveillance Bureau. Not at all, they preach meditation and vegetarianism, the call came from a Dr Francisco Ripalda, who's here from Mexico City and was going to stay with the deceased; write down the address and get going.

He knew the neighbourhood of Guadalupe fairly well. Split down the middle by Obregón Avenue, it lay below La Lomita church and to one side of the Col Pop, where he had lived for his entire life.

In the living room sat Dr Ripalda, plus a thin man and two women, one of whom looked particularly shaken. They were drinking lemonade. Mendieta and Zelda observed the scene for a moment, then sat down with them. An impossible case? I hope so, the detective took out his PalmPilot and straightened his legs, when there is a body to contend with the living are more important than the dead. On the wall hung landscapes, a few diplomas from the U.S.B., a painting by María Romero depicting a woman's genitals, and another by Kijano. Who found him? While Ripalda raised his hand, Mendieta observed the others. Three potted plants gave the room a comfy feel.

We are members of the Universal Small Brotherhood, which Attorney Canizales also belonged to; I live in Mexico City, but I'm giving a course on transcendental meditation and I've been coming here weekends for the past month, the attorney always picks me up at the airport and I stay here; this morning when he did not meet me and didn't answer his telephone I took a taxi; the door was open and I found him on his bed, aren't you going to look at the body? because besides the door I haven't touched a thing. Did you call these people? I called Señor Figueroa, he indicated the thin man, who is our leader here. And what did you do? I telephoned Laura and Dania so they would keep me company, I'm rather sensitive and I didn't dare come by myself, I still haven't the courage to look at him, he gestured towards the bedroom at the back. And you? Laura Frías wiped away a tear. We went in to see him. Besides being in the U.S.B. together, is there anything else? We were like brothers and sisters, he always stood by us. Dania Estrada had a lovely voice. Laura simply nodded. By the way, we called his family in Navolato and they'll be here soon. What time was it when you found him? About 8.20. Did he live alone? Yes, sir. Did you visit him often? Not really, Figueroa said, we'd see him at our centre, which is on Riva Palacio Street. We girls saw him last week, we had tea at the Verdi and we talked. About what? About his plans, about the news that he'd been nominated for professional of the year, he wanted to go back to the Safety Council to put an end to the violence. Really? the detective smiled, did he work? At Social Security, he was a legal adviser. The car in the garage, is that his? They nodded. Do you have any idea who killed him? They shook their heads. O.K., give your addresses, telephones, and cell phone numbers to Agent Toledo in case we need you for any clarifications, he made a quick note on his Palm; the technical people will be here soon, they'll take your fingerprints just in case you touched anything else.

He opened the door with a handkerchief. He closed his eyes and concentrated. Aromas assaulted his senses and were on the point of evoking a memory: what is that dry, spicy fragrance?

He observed the body on the twisted sheets, the bloodstain. Black pants, white shirt, dark socks. The bullet hole was in the left temple. The detective took in the tidiness of the room, no mess on the floor or on the furniture. Thursday's newspapers lay on a leather easy chair. On the chest of drawers, the novel *News from the Empire* by Fernando del Paso. He took photographs with his cell phone. Using a Kleenex he picked up the remote and turned the television on: Channel 22, the favourite of the culture-loving middle class. "Every Wednesday at 8.30 p.m. 'Caught in Fiction,' interviews with the authors of the latest in Mexican literature", an advertising voice intoned. He turned it off. Under the bed he saw black shoes, a pair of sandals, and at the back a square object. He moved the bed: it was another copy of *News from the Empire*. He did not touch it. Two copies: a reader? One entire wall was covered by bookshelves, which as far as he could tell were filled with contemporary literature. Carefully, he opened the closet, also a model of perfect order. Typical, an example to us all, I swear I'll be the same when I grow up. Shirts, pants, and suits hung in an impeccable line, polished shoes all in their places. From the window he looked out at the back yard: plants, a clothesline, a few used tyres. The bathroom was immaculate: bathrobe, towels, soaps, colognes. He breathed in. The spicy aroma did not emanate from there. He looked at his watch: 10.58. He took a few pictures with the cell and went back into the bedroom.

Zelda came in and stared at the cadaver: In a minute the techies will be here and also someone from the district attorney's office, Mendieta sniffed the sheets, he was thirty-seven years old, single, the son of Hildegardo Canizales. The former minister of agriculture, she added, the detective looked again at his watch, she moved close to the wound. And he was handsome, she scrutinised the hole in his head and then the carpet. Did you see this, boss? She pointed at the shoes, a pair of black loafers. What? They look a lot alike, but they're different. Mendieta squatted and saw she was right. You are a genius, Zelda, we'll have to watch out the Russians don't grab you, one is even cleaner than the other. He called Dr Montaño's cell.

We're in Guadalupe near Río Piaxtla, get over here right away. What, weren't you in Piggyback? Yeah, only that body got up to have another drink. I'll be there in fifteen minutes. Half an hour, thought the detective, and he asked Zelda to step out. Sister, go see the neighbours, ask them the usual, see if anybody agrees to tell you anything.

Montaño was a rather libertine young doctor, early that morning he had called to say he would send two students to Piggyback, since at that moment he was in a darkened room making a fool of himself with a cheerleader for the Culiacán Tomateros. Do me a favour, Lefty, I promise to be all yours at eleven. You give me your word? I swear, have I ever let you down? As predicted, half an hour later he appeared accompanied by the same technicians from Forensic

Services who had worked on the gangsta-wrap: Dudes, the shoes are from different pairs, there are two copies of the same book, check them out then give them to me, find his cell phone, get me the calls from the past week. He's the son of a former federal minister and he's a former member of the Citizens' Safety Council, I'm telling you so you won't just fill out the form. Where's Ortega? He's at Head-quarters. The doctor took a look at the body and nodded, stuck in the thermometer: Body temperature drops one degree every hour, so he's been dead five to seven hours. He moved the head. The bullet went out by his right ear and if they killed him here it should be around. Anything else before the autopsy? Nothing for certain. Don't you smell something funny? Montaño smiled: Right now I still smell of my lovely little girl, but maybe they sprayed something on him, I'll let you know. He agreed to call later on. Then, without taking his eyes off Zelda, who had not gone out as he had asked, Montaño came up to him and made a sign of what about her, Mendieta let him know the way was clear, Montaño, all smiles, gave him the Roman thumbs up.

Cavalry charge. It was Briseño: Hurry it up, don't do an autopsy, get ballistics and forensics to work quickly. What's the problem? That's what his father wants, Engineer Canizales, the former agri-culture minister; District Attorney Bracamontes just called me to say we should expedite it all and hand over the body as soon as the family turns up. Even if it has murder written all over it? It doesn't matter, consider it natural causes. O.K. He gave the order to Montaño and the techies, who accepted it as a matter of course. In their departments anything could happen and everything did. they ended up just dusting for fingerprints.

They were leaving when the family lawyer arrived with one of the brothers. The father was in the United States negotiating the price of corn for the region's farmers and would not be back until the funeral, the mother did not have the courage to come and swallow this bitter pill. Instead of speaking with them, the detective asked Zelda to get their basics and to set up a date with the parents. Then he took Laura Frías to the Miró, which he preferred to his tiny office at Headquarters.

Why her? Such sadness, there had to be a reason.

Four

Paola drank beer from a can and looked out the window at her longtime neighbourhood. Eyes dry, dull, blank. She had turned all the photographs and paintings in her room to face the wall. Except the one of her parents at their twenty-fifth wedding anniversary, which was on the dressing table next to two empty beer cans. Bookshelf full. It was 8.10 a.m. and the house was as quiet as could be. No-one nearby, no-one moving. No-one was her sister Beatriz, her brother Dante, and her parents.

She thought when it comes to dying, every day is the same, who wants to live for ever? She once slept with an undertaker who liked to say that. Living or dying makes no difference, only the former happens at 7.00 and the latter at 7.30.

Afraid? She had sworn to it so many times, she did not even feel upset. She would do just as she had said and that way she would not have to answer any questions or put up with the black walls of the days to come.

The grey sky was appropriate.

The neighbourhood had always seemed horrible to her, no personality, awful narrow steep streets. From her window on the second floor she saw a young man on a bicycle come out and glide downhill. For a moment she saw him in her arms and she recognised herself in his kisses, but she wiped that away immediately. She did not like anyone in the neighbourhood and even less a boy who thought he could win her heart and her charm with beer and wheedling flattery. Idiot, nothing means nothing.

What a difference. Bruno's kisses were soft, no drooling saliva, not always the same. She met him when the University of Sinaloa gave an honorary doctorate to Carlos Fuentes. They were both in line to get their books signed and they talked about what they thought of them. She had four and he had them all. After the writer signed and chatted with them both, they went to have a juice because he did not drink. That was when they kissed the first time and he said he was one of those who never marries. That was also their first night together.

The bedroom was large. Off-white. Beside the window a black computer on a table laden with books and notebooks. Her bag was on the dressing table, next to three unopened cans of beer and surrounded by bottles of perfume and a bedraggled teddy bear. She went over, in the mirror she looked uncombed and determined. She opened the bag and reached for the pistol. A final message? She felt a tiny impulse when she saw the lipstick, but she controlled herself. What for? She put the photograph of her parents face down. She turned on the television, Channel 22 was broadcasting a round table on contemporary art, lay down on the bed, and shot herself in the right temple.

In the street the kid with the bike, who had returned, looked at Paola's window without comprehending, made a move towards the house, then stopped, he let a few seconds go by, waved his arm, spun around, and went into his own home.

Did you see "The Good, the Bad and the Ugly"? That music crossed the young man's mind.

Five

Laura Frías came back from the ladies' room lightly made up: red lips, pleasant face. Sadness had laid waste to her black eyes and the timbre of her voice. Thin. She was wearing light-blue pants and a white blouse. Mendieta liked that, a woman who thinks of her appearance is at least a dreamer. Chestnut hair to her collar and a certain mischievousness around her mouth. They ate, she a Caesar salad with extra dressing, he Black Forest on a baguette, orange juice and coffee. She told him she lived alone, had studied psychology, and loved the simple life. In 1900 she would have been happy working as a nurse, wearing those uniforms that came down to your ankles, eating vegetables grown without fertilisers. No doubt you would have been Porfirio Díaz's lover, and he wouldn't have let you eat this for breakfast. I also wouldn't be suffering about Bruno, she turned to look at the coffee grinder a few steps from the table, even if I don't like the stuff I love that aroma. Were you really just friends? Yes, even if that seems strange to you, why do men always think there's more? Don't women? It depends. Where did he have his office? At Social Security, we told you, he was a legal adviser. Do you know if he went to work yesterday? He was always working, he was ground to a powder by the end of the week. Did he have an assistant? Mónica Alfaro, a lawyer. Mendieta called Angelita, his secretary, and asked her to find out what time Canizales had left the office the day before. Who do you think killed him?

He was a friend, a true friend, his life was unlucky, but it shouldn't have ended like that, two tears rolled down her cheeks, she looked again at the coffee grinder, he was kind, attentive, generous; several times I asked him to straighten up, I knew his wild ways would not lead to anything good, especially in his case since people in the U.S.B. looked up to him, his family, too; he only smiled, I think deep down he hated peace and quiet and preferred strong emotions, things that overwhelm you and keep you on edge; for about six months he had a girlfriend, a beautiful but tempestuous girl with a suicidal urge; her name is Paola Rodríguez, twice I heard her threaten to kill him and then kill herself if he ever left her, incredibly demanding, when he finally did it was a big drama, she'd turn up at his house at three in the morning, she'd show up at his parties, find him at his office, at the movies; she would not leave him alone; one day we were at the Chuparrosa Enamorada and she threatened to take off all her clothes right there if he wouldn't go someplace with her I can't remember where; that's how she took it, poor woman, until she finally calmed down; I think she still called him now and again, but you could say she'd decided to leave him be. Hmm. He was also involved with Samantha Valdés, the widow of a narco that got killed in Nogales, you must know about that, I think he was with the Camargos; at first Bruno seemed happy, as I said he liked to live on the edge, he lived for excitement, but later on when her father sent his thugs to threaten him he tried to put some distance between them; I don't know how much he managed to, the girl is strong-willed, she's got a seven-year-old boy who adored him; once one of the bodyguards put an A.K. to his head, he told them it was not his doing, they should talk to her so she wouldn't chase after him, but the guy said if he continued seeing her they'd blow him to kingdom come; Samantha's bisexual, some time later a woman turned up at his house and threatened him the same way, if she found out he was bothering her girl he'd find out who she was, her name is Mariana Kelly; he was scared, I think she drew a pistol on him; he was bisexual too, for long periods he was totally in love with a stupendous dancer, Frank Aldana, they had a relationship, but he always went back to the girls and Frank would fall apart, he'd cry, he'd threaten, poor guy, he'd whine about Bruno's lack of commitment and all that he made him suffer; as you can see, Bruno led a pretty dynamic life.

Who nominated him for professional of the year? The Law Society he belonged to. How long was he on the Citizens' Safety Council? Not long, maybe three months, he crossed somebody and figured it was better to get out, he was an idealist that way, he believed he could put an end to the violence. Who did he have trouble with? I never knew. He asked for another juice.

The Miró was full of housewives talking in loud voices.

Is Samantha the daughter of Marcelo Valdés? No more, no less; I saw her once in the Arcos, we were celebrating my birthday when she came in with two men, they sat in a corner peaceably enough and the bodyguards came in right after, we thought they would close down the restaurant and pay all the bills like they say they do, but no, everything was normal as could be, they ate and they left without any fuss. Who do you think killed Bruno? Isn't it your job to figure that out? I have nothing to go on, but you do; since it happened in his bedroom, barefoot but with his clothes on, and everything neat and tidy, it could have been someone he trusted. Well, you tell me, of all the ones I've mentioned which one do you like? Maybe he had new friends? I didn't meet any. Just what does Ripalda do? What he said, he gives courses on meditation. Why did he stay with Canizales? To save money, the U.S.B. is not an organisation with a lot of resources, her expression was frank and she spoke with confidence. What about Figueroa? He just administers the U.S.B., he's a good yoga teacher. Give me the telephone numbers of these people. I don't have them, but they must be in Bruno's appointment book, look for it in his briefcase, which he usually left in the car, I brought it to him several times. Did you stay at his house? Many times, listen, when are they going to hand over the body? the brother and the family lawyer are coming for it and you know they don't live here. Do you know them? I went with Bruno to his parents' house a few times, it's a mansion in the middle of an orchard. How did Bruno get along with them? His father was sort of stubborn, but his mother adored him; he had no problems with his brother.

He called Zelda: Look in Canizales's appointment book or on his cell phone for the telephones of the following people. He read out the list. Boss, Dr Montaño already worked it out with the family lawyer, he's about to give them the body, the funeral home people have been here for a while, the techies all left. Did they look at the car? I don't know. O.K., I'll see you in a little while. He hung up; so, in what way was Bruno an example to his family? His only brother followed in his footsteps and became a lawyer. Did they work together? No, Joaquín takes care of the family business. But they have a lawyer. Attorney Beltrán, someone Bruno detested, he said he was just a crook; can I go? Where do you work? I'm a masseuse. Really? Don't get excited, commander, I'm the kind who keeps her clothes on, I work by appointment and I need to cancel

31

today's to deal with Bruno, my office is downtown, on Buelna. I'll give you a lift, she was a woman who smiled with her eyes.

She went off to the ladies' room again and he wrote in his Palm: "bisexual, spatial intell, Aldan, S Vald, Mariana K, Paola Rod, Yoonohoo V". The cavalry charge rang out on his cell phone. It was Zelda: Write these down, boss, oh, and regarding the neighbours three are farmers and went out early, the others neither heard nor saw anything, generally speaking they liked Canizales, he gave more than one of them advice on legal matters.

Before Laura returned, he reached Beatriz Rodríguez, who said her sister had committed suicide. When? This morning, around eight o'clock.

Six

Samantha arrived early at her parents' house in Colinas de San Miguel, a fortress with a flower garden in full bloom. She found them staring at a skimpy breakfast. I can hardly believe it, she kissed each on the forehead. And my darling? I just left him at school, what happened, why the big change? she gestured at the chunks of pineapple and the limp nopales. Nothing, just that yesterday we went to see Dr Elenes and he put your father on a diet. But you aren't fat. I'm bordering on diabetic and my weight is bothering my right knee, he took an apple from the fruit bowl and bit into it. I hope you can get by without your pork rinds and your seafood. His cholesterol came out high too. That's no big deal. But you're going to take care of yourself, my love, you promised; now, daughter would you like some breakfast? But ma, there's nothing wrong with me. I'll tell Genoveva to make you something good. I'd like chorizo and scrambled eggs. Marcelo Valdés and his first-born daughter were left alone, the breakfast room was small, it had a cuckoo clock and two sideboards filled with silverware and an assortment of knick-knacks. I came to tell you that they killed Bruno Canizales; through the window they could see two guards seated on a log in the huge garden, relaxed in conversation. Did we do it? Tany Contreras made the trip from Nogales and you know he never misses. The old man shook his head, disapproving. Pa, it was necessary, he had me at the end of my rope, besides, you intimidated him several times, don't you remember? When you speak to me, do so properly, don't

33

you forget that you owe me respect and that this is an honourable home, his pale face had turned bright red; to waste powder on a little nuisance is reckless and stupid, this will be the last time you take care of somebody without my consent, and start behaving like a decent woman, don't think I approve of the life you lead, his expression was dark, and if I had any dealings with him it was to protect you, don't forget that I am on good terms with his father. Minerva returned: My love, what's wrong, oh God Almighty, I think his blood sugar's up again, remember you're not supposed to get upset, did you say something to him? Nothing. Well, I'll have to take him to Tucson because this is not normal, she made him drink water, I'm going to call the doctor right now. Take it easy, I'll go into the garden and get some air and I'll feel better, leave the doctor be, no-one dies this early in the day, he stood up, he was wearing a white shirt and khaki pants. Don't talk nonsense, aren't you going to keep Samantha company while she eats? You sit with her, I'm going outside. About 160 centimetres tall and weighing ninety kilos, he walked slowly out and towards a small bungalow surrounded by bushes about ten metres from the house. As soon as the hired guns spotted him they got to their feet. Although the boss was looking feeble of late, they knew he could easily make half the country tremble and that even the weather sought his advice.

Inside, Samantha was talking on her cell phone. Smiling, relaxed. Her features soft, lovely. She hung up when her mother came in with a full plate and a mug of coffee.

Seven

He parked in front of the house where the kid with the bike lived, three cars filled the Rodríguez's side of the street. The garage, empty. The kid with the bike was leaning against one of the cars, he told him he had heard the gunshot and it had worried him. Around here we were all in love with her. Was she that good-looking? She was the law, the queen of the good and the bad. And who was the stud? She wouldn't give us the time of day, she got her kicks someplace else and with somebody else, though people all said the stud was the one who's talking. Oh, yeah? My miserable heart would have given anything. Couldn't one of the lovesick guys she sent packing have killed her? Not anybody from around here, we're not idiots, a body as perfect as hers is worth nothing underground. O.K., your loyalty and good taste are duly noted, did you see any new pretenders? you know they're never lacking. Not often, whenever one turned up we'd beat the shit out of him and it worked like a charm. What about the lawyer, Canizales? Just let that asshole show his face, more than a few of us have sworn to take him out. Save me his guts. Let's see if the dogs leave any.

Good afternoon. I'm Edgar Mendieta from the State Ministerial Police. Pale-green room, stereo, family photographs, a dining table for ten, kitchen at the back. To one side, the father's office with the door ajar. The mother was sitting on the sofa, sobbing, Dante was working a Rubik's cube with surprising skill, and Beatriz was looking at her hands. Come in. The body had been taken to the funeral home and that's where the father was. This is the man who called before, clarified Beatriz, a 28-year-old with blonde curly hair, what can I get you?

She took him to the bedroom on the second floor, the bed now perfectly made, bloodstain on the pillow, where her sister had committed suicide. From the moment he walked in, the scent of Carolina Herrera struck him, he had caught a whiff of it in Canizales' bedroom too. He wrote on the Palm: "Perf. Car. Herrer also in Caniz rm?" Why did she turn the pictures around? The beers had grown warm, the midday light filtered through gauze curtains. I have no idea, he thought about calling Ortega but then thought better of it. Where's the gun? It was waiting wrapped in a pink towel in a closet jam-packed with dresses, blouses, and a mess of shoes and boxes in a heap. He put the pistol in the right-hand pocket of his jacket, in the left pocket he had his own, he looked at the books and wrote down a few things. I put the bullet there, she pointed at the computer keyboard, Mendieta wrapped it in a Kleenex and put it with the gun. Shall we turn the pictures back? Beatriz agreed. They were lithographs of places and famous paintings: "The Scream", "The Nude Maja", "The Two Fridas". Two photographs with Bruno Canizales, the rest with relatives and friends. He had no trouble seeing what a beauty she was: delicate features, perfect mouth, lips slightly puckered, a redhead with curly hair, enigmatic gaze. What a pity, he agreed with the kid.

Do you know this man? Of course, Bruno Canizales, my sister was crazy about him, if you ask me why she did what she did, it was for him; they were together for a while, but he was a bit off, some days you couldn't believe his good vibes, he'd talk with you, he'd get excited about whatever you were interested in, he'd give advice, then other days just the opposite: a closed book, turned in on himself; Papa never trusted him, when they were together he'd visit us twice a week; she was strange, even when she was little, if she wanted anything from Papa she would say she was going to kill herself, she liked to take over, to be the centre of attention; when we grew up she turned moody, unpredictable, volatile; I didn't get it, because she had everything: beauty, intelligence, friends, all the money she needed; she could be a good sister, too, though usually she was a mystery; after Bruno we didn't meet anybody else; the truth is the boys were all over her, a narco from Badiraguato even hired a band to serenade her once, but she was stuck on Canizales and no-one could get her off him. Was she very passionate? More like obsessive, she would get hooked on an idea and no human power could make her change her mind. On anything at all? It was her way of relating to people. What did she like to watch on television? Concerts, interviews, boring things they say cultured people like, Channel 22 from Mexico City. How did she get along with the bros from around here? Some of them were nuts about her, but I don't think she picked up on anyone. Do you know who sold her the pistol? No, the pistol belongs to Papa, she must have taken it at some point. Did she work? No, Papa gives us everything. Yesterday did she do anything different? Her usual routine, she spent all day here reading and listening to music, I went out at 6.40 in the evening and she was still in her pyjamas; when I came back at about 11.30, I saw her dressed, having a supper of sweet buns and hot milk, as if she were just getting in, and I saw nothing more until morning when I heard the shot. Did you notice if she went out later? No, at least I didn't hear her, after she and Bruno broke up she drank a lot, she wouldn't get drunk, but she'd always be drinking. Where did she buy the beers? At the Oxxo or wherever. Mendieta saw a plain white plastic bag on the floor next to the dresser. I'm going to take this. Go ahead. So you think she did it for Canizales. I don't know, one day she did tell him in front of me: If you dump me I'll kill myself. I'm also going to take along the empty cans, using a Kleenex he put them in the plastic bag.

What would you think if you knew that Bruno Canizales was found dead this morning? They looked at each other: she was lovely too, honey-coloured eyes and a mole on her cheek; him a normal 43-year-old police officer, always dressed in black, three days without shaving, and incapable of falling in love. Is it true? He nodded, I heard that she threatened to kill him then take her own life if he left her. I know she blackmailed him like that, the way I told you I heard her say once, what I don't know is if she would dare do it, you know, the first part; she had terrific days when she was relaxed and happy, a person who brought joy into your life just by walking by, my father adored her, my mother was jealous, we didn't know what to feel about her, especially over the past few months when it was hard to read her heart. What do you do? I'm an actress, even though I don't look it, we've got a show on now, that's why I came home yesterday when I did.

Calvary charge. Mendieta. What's up, bonehead, you must be scratching your balls as usual. It was Guillermo Ortega, head of Criminal Investigation Services. What a crock of shit, what did you find? What do you mean what did I find? come on, the guilty party of course, I always find the culprit and don't you forget it; listen, my boys located the shell case and the slug and you aren't going to believe me, Canizales was killed with a 9mm Smith & Wesson and the bullet was made of silver. What do you make of that? The jerk was probably a vampire. Where did they find it? Among the sheets, it's a little squashed, there's a small dent in the wall where it hit before falling onto the bed. So they killed him standing up. That's most likely, then they laid him down so you could take his picture. And what's up with the shoes? One is expensive, the other is Chinese masquerading as Italian, you can get them in the Izábal Market, both of them were down at the heel. And the prints? We're working on it, you know we didn't get to do a complete check, however, everything seems to point to a case of Jack the Ripper. Just what I feared, have you had a chance to look at his cell phone, I need the calls from the last week at least. Lefty, are you an idiot or what? you think we're machines? Got the message, I'll look for you later, he hung up, he knew that any case that did not move quickly would get dropped and he was liking this one.

Forgive me, the technical guy can't live without me; from Paola's bag he pulled out a cell phone on a little chain, we'll check her calls and give it back to you, O.K.? Keep it, I don't think any of us would want to use it. Which is Paola's car? The grey Ford, do you want to see it? I do. He put the white plastic bag in the Jetta. The car was open, the kid with the bike looked on from the doorway of his house. Beatriz smiled at him. Tank almost empty, dirty paper napkins and Kleenex, flyers, a book of stories by Eduardo Antonio Parra, three pairs of shoes, an umbrella, a Post-it with the U.R.L.s for Cristina Rivera Garza's and Rafa Saavedra's blogs. The floor on the passenger side had a bit of fresh mud. That could be the footprint of the last person who saw her alive, it was still drizzling, when did it start? He remembered seeing a cloudy sky when he left Dr Parra's office. In the glove compartment nothing of interest. Is all this necessary? Beatriz asked. No, it's routine, he noted something on the Palm, she had a connection with Canizales, now the two of them are dead, and we have to take that into account; did Paola see the play you are in? I'm not sure, she never mentioned it, but I think I saw her there on opening night.

They went back to the house. Dante had not even heard the gunshot and the mother could not stop weeping because for a whole month she had refused to speak a word to her now-dead daughter. I could never make my darling girl understand how much I loved her. You're a heavy sleeper, the detective said to Dante who was still working the Rubik's cube. I got home late. What time? About 4.30. Was it raining? Drizzling. Did you see a light on in her room? I didn't notice, but her car was in the street and usually she puts it in the garage; the windshield was wet, which indicates that the probability she had turned on the wipers is low. That's reasonable. More than reasonable, it's probable, and it's also probable that she had gone out and was going to go out again. Mendieta nodded approvingly, the young man kept on at the cube. What do you study? Mathematics.

When he was getting into the Jetta the kid with the bike came over: Take me prisoner, copper, because I'm going to kill the culprit. It was suicide. But it was because of a jerk who screwed her around, I swear that asshole won't see daylight tomorrow. What asshole? That dickhead of a lawyer. Ah, kid, they beat you to it, he met the dawn with a bullet hole in his head. No kidding. Don't ask, and who the hell are you? No big deal, I'm head of the club in love with the queen and I'm the son of my mother. Well, things moved on, dude, they left you fanning the breeze.

He called Zelda Toledo: Did you contact Alfaro at Social Security? Yup, she said that Canizales had no problems with his bosses or with the union, that he was a good lawyer who kept everything in order; they were surprised to learn he was dead. You don't say, now find out what time the drizzle started in the East Sector. Where's that? Around Ernesto Millán Park. I'm seeing him now, copper, one of those wise guys, the ones who always get their way. What are you trying to tell me? Just that, my copper, and that I'm disgusted they beat me to it. Don't jump into a fight you maybe can't punch your way out of. I couldn't care less, I don't give a fuck about anything, sweet fuck all, less than sweet fuck all, whatever, like she used to say . . . he jerked his head towards Paola's house.

Mendieta got into the car and drove off. "There is a house in New Orleans," maestro Eric Burdon sang.

He took Zapata Boulevard all the way to San Chelín Funeral Home.

Abelardo Rodríguez, the father, agreed to talk to the detective there and then. They sat down in a couple of white chairs. You have no idea how this is going to affect our lives, she was our sun, our compass. He was smoking cigarillos. He pulled out a hip flask and poured whisky into two plastic cups. Not only was she lovely, she was highly intelligent, she never tried to use her beauty to get ahead, in contests or anything, never, not even in school, she was a girl who knew what she wanted, she was too restless, she had everything to live for, my mind can't grasp why she would do such a thing. How did she get hold of your pistol? He showed him the Beretta. That's something I can't stop asking myself, when did my daughter take that gun without me noticing, I don't know and you can't imagine how much that pains me. Is it registered? Somewhere I must have the permit, it runs out next month. If it's no bother, I'd like to see it within three days. None at all, I'll go by the station and drop it off for you. Mendieta told him about Canizales. No kidding, he was such a nice guy I thought he would live for ever, what's more he was a very good lawyer, I had the pleasure of meeting his father, Engineer Hildegardo Canizales, a stupendous person; I liked him for my daughter, but God didn't want them to get along, and now all this, it's true what they say about misfortune never turning up alone. Señor Rodríguez, I need to have my technicians do a couple of things, we won't be a bother, I'll take the pistol so they can check it and the forensic doctor will take a look at your daughter's body. That's fine, just one favour I'd ask, no sacrilege, please, I don't want them poking around her private parts. You can be sure they won't. There was a pause, Rodríguez poured one more for himself, the detective had not touched his. Well look, detective, whatever we can do for you, don't hesitate, Christ, after all the guy was practically my son-in-law. What play is your daughter Beatriz in? A piece of shit, listen, I don't even know what it's called, he finished his drink and poured another, all I can say is she goes on stage indecent, something Paola never would have done.

Mendieta hurried his own and went to the toilet. He used the cell phone: Montaño, get yourself over here to San Chelín right away, they're preparing the body of one of the suspects and I need to know if it has semen. Lefty, don't do this to me, I'm on the road to paradise with the most beautiful and sexy woman I have ever met. Is this your week for a double-header? Something like that. Well, leave it for later, this is urgent, before the funeral home people get to her; go in the service entrance. Then he called Ortega and asked him to send a technician to look for gunpowder on her hands.

After that, without the father noticing, he slipped into the embalming room, where they knew him. Well, slackers, are you behaving yourselves? Marvellously. His eyes paused on Paola's face, so lovely not even the post-mortem pallor diminished it. Chief, did you lose something? This babe killed herself, before you open her up I'd like Montaño to see her, I need to know a few things. Ooh, you need to keep an eye on that guy, they smirked, he's wild. You take charge of that, that's why it's on your turf.

Cavalry charge. His secretary Angelita gave him the news that Attorney Canizales had been at work at Social Security on Thursday from eight in the morning until six in the evening without breaking for lunch. Could he have been plotting something against the union? those guys also find time to rub people out.

He went back to the father, who immediately offered him another drink. Mendieta could see the aura of sadness through the fumes from the alcohol and the cigarillo. He worked in construction, that was why he had guns. Now with the crisis everything has ground to a halt, for example I couldn't pay for my daughter to do a graduate degree in Spain, if I'd had the cash for that maybe this wouldn't have happened; she probably would have been able to withstand Canizales dumping her; I never understood the man, imagine daring to leave a girl of that calibre. Señor Rodríguez, there are more stupid people than we think. He was fifty-two and in his youth he'd made it as a midfielder with Chivas in Guadalajara, but he missed his family too much and after three months he quit. His office was in the Tenth Lot, just this side of Piggyback.

Thirty-eight minutes later, Montaño called from the room next door. Positive result, Lefty my man, I'll take a sample with me and write up the record in case you need it; we also found gunpowder on her right hand; listen, what perfection, eh? I've been asking myself where she could have been hiding that I never met her. Thank you, doctor, see you later; Señor Rodríguez, the forensic doctor is finished, I've got to get going, the technicians will analyse the pistol and when you bring me the permit I'll return it to you. Mendieta preferred tequila, but he had no problem saying "your health" again, it was a way of consoling the afflicted father. What do you think of Smith & Wessons, Señor Rodríguez? Fine, but I'm loyal to Sergeant Pietro Beretta. They said goodbye.

At a seafood stand, he ate fish ceviche and shrimp with octopus, and had a tamarind juice before going on to Headquarters.

Eight

Gringo, you work for me, you have no business carrying out my daughter's caprices, let this be the last time you eliminate someone without my consent, especially when it has nothing to do with the business; if I asked you to threaten him a couple of times that means nothing and you ought to know that; I am on good terms with his father and it is going to hurt me if he finds out that one of my men was behind the murder of his son. They were in a small and stuffy office at the back of the residence, crowded with a tiny desk, a couple of chairs, a bar-fridge, and a safe that rarely held any money. Marcelo Valdés always put things where they belonged. But Don Marcelo. Shut up, he threw a paperweight at him and it struck him in the chest, the one in charge around here is me, the one who does the talking is me, the one who gives the orders is me; I know you brought Tany Contreras in for the job, so send him back to Nogales and tell him to stay put until I give the order, what kind of stupidity is that to use silver bullets? what, the guy was a vampire? because his family is unimpeachable. I didn't know. . . Shut your mouth I'm telling you, he threw a statuette at him. Actually we haven't paid Tany. You figure that out, I don't plan to give you a single peso. Ernesto Ponce, the Gringo: forty-two years old, tall, strong, with white skin and blue eyes, a gold bracelet on each wrist and four diamond rings; he wore a blue silk shirt and classic Levi's, ostrich-leather cowboy boots. Change the guards, this morning I saw them sitting on the log chewing the fat while who knows what could have been happening outside, they're of no use to me, I need people with eagle eyes and the bodies of sharks. A knock. Who is it? My love, they're calling you from Mexico City. He made a sign to the Gringo to open the door and get lost, his wife handed him a cordless telephone. Hello? He listened for a few moments. Tell the honourable minister that I will not invest in that, I am not interested in the soft-drink industry, and if he continues harassing me I will take my money out of the country and put it in Costa Rica or wherever, we'll see who loses more, goodnight, he hung up; that idiot, what's going on? they give him a post and he thinks the Virgin speaks to him, I spent years greasing his palm and now he wants to lean on me; what he is he owes to me and he hasn't a clue how money is made. My life, my love, don't get upset, remember what the doctor said, there was a brief silence. I want to disappear, go away someplace where nobody knows me, what, do they want to see me dead? well they're the ones who'll be fucked. Calm down, my love, tomorrow I'll go pray to Malverde and I'll take him our donation, but calm down, would you like to have supper now? He closed his eyes, I'd like a steak with a nice guacamole and a cold beer, he leaned back in his easy chair. That's not good for you, my king, wait until you're better and I'll make it just the way you like it; oh yes, two ladies from El Potrero de los Rivas came by. Yeah? A village near my mother's home. What did they want? Could you bring in electric lights and could we help restore the church, it's falling down. You take care of that, get the electricity put in right away, and fix up the school too. You are a saint, my love. Mmm.

Nine

Cavalry charge. He was driving down Zapata Boulevard towards his office listening to a news flash from the journalist Quiroz: "Found dead this morning, murdered at his home in this city's Guadalupe neighbourhood, was Attorney Bruno Canizales, nominee for professional of the year and eldest son of Engineer Hildegardo Canizales, minister of agriculture in the government of Alonso Trujillo. He had a bullet hole in his head and an empty 9mm shell was found; the police, this station has learned, are chasing down two clues that are certain to lead them to the murderers. For 'Eyes on the Night' this is Daniel Quiroz reporting." Mendieta, he barked. What a delight to hear your voice, kiddo. Who's talking? What do you mean who's talking, I thought you'd be jumping for joy. Look, I'm in Cinépolis in the middle of a shootout, call me in three hours. Right, I won't curse your mother because we have the same one. Enrique? I haven't heard that you've got another brother, asshole, unless our mother rose from the dead and our father finally turned up after forty years, is it true about the shootout? because I can't hear shit. An old trick. Well, you've got good aim, how are you? Rolling in glory, and you? Same as always, up to my ears in work but I'm good, his brother had gone away after his lover had died and for twelve years he had been living in Oregon, how are my hometown girls? Culiacán girls are great, you know they're our pride and our perdition. You can't imagine how much I think about them. So, come back, what are you doing over there? do you remember the son of Doña Librada, that nutcase

47

who was your buddy? How could I not remember my pal Teo. Well, he said to hell with everything on the other side of the border, he bought a rig, and he's driving around the country; he takes loads from Tijuana to Veracruz, from Culiacán to Laredo, and all over. Well, one of these days I'll do something like that, how's the Col Pop? Better than ever. Can you still score weed on the corner? Sure. O.K., I just called to see how you were, since you're incapable of doing it. I appreciate it, truly. And what about your love life, kiddo? I'll tell you about that some other time. That means you're cold; don't get stuck, remember love is renewable, any nail will pull out a tack. I'm alright, you'll see when I tell you about it, do you think the Culiacán girls would let somebody like me be alone for long? No, that's true, they must be tearing each other's hair out over your bones. More or less. What about the blonde? Later, I tell you, how's Isabel? We're fine, going to fat but nothing else; O.K., kiddo, say hello to the bros and take care of yourself.

Briseño's cubicle had his name printed on an acrylic strip glued to the door. Lefty went in. The chief, an overweight 36-year-old, was drinking coffee and smoking unfiltered cigarettes. Family connections more than smarts or accomplishments had landed him the job. The detective sat down and waited for him to finish speaking on the telephone with his wife; he was giving her a recipe for fish wrapped in tinfoil he had found on the Internet. Photographs and certificates on the walls. Desk covered in documents and the computer turned on. No, my love, he shouted, not mustard, no, do it the way I said, and he hung up.

What's up, Mendieta, how is it going with the Bruno Canizales case? We're interrogating those involved, and as good luck would have it Paola Rodríguez, the principal suspect, committed suicide. Don't forget who he is the son of, this is your chance. Chance for what? Don't you want a promotion? No. What about this fine parchment? he threw a bulging brown envelope onto the desk. That I would like, they smiled, the detective put it in his pants pocket. Then he gave a quick overview of the day's events. What's your theory, Lefty? As of now none, given how tidy it all was it doesn't appear to be a crime of passion. Me, I'm inclined towards vengeance, the commander said; you know, straightening things up could just be a cover; his father is dreaming about the big chair in the presidential palace and that brings enemies out of the woodwork, the silver bullet might indicate the social standing of the killer. I'll keep that in mind, too bad we couldn't go over the crime scene carefully, remember you ordered us out. Lefty, don't go all rhetorical on me, I'm sure you saw enough; besides Rodríguez, who else have you turned up? He told him. No doubt about it, you are a lucky man, you detest the narcos and the biggest of them all drops onto your chest; don't hesitate, go get Marcelo Valdés and get his daughter too, and if they're off travelling, go wherever you have to. Briseño's cell phone rang, he saw it was his home number. How does it look? perfect, now keep it on low for forty-four minutes, the detective stood up, Mendieta, he insisted covering the mouthpiece, this is your opportunity, don't blow it, and he continued the conversation with his wife, no, my love, you don't make sweetcorn soup that way, what sort of mother did you have?

He called Zelda Toledo into his tiny office. On the shamelessly peeling wall hung three diplomas that Angelita dusted with devotion and a Coppel department store calendar from the previous year. He brought her up to date: his chat with Laura Frías, Paula's suicide, the silver bullet. She'd never heard of anyone being killed with a silver bullet. Haven't you ever seen a vampire movie? No. Well, you ought to, he gave her Paola Rodríguez's cell phone, find out who she called the day before she died and if Ortega doesn't get a move on you'll have to get Canizales' back from him, maybe it still has a record of the outgoing and incoming calls; find Frank Aldana, and we also have to interview Samantha Valdés, Mariana Kelly and Marcelo Valdés. They fell silent, voices drifted in from the hallway. They're everywhere, aren't they? Mendieta nodded, and you have to interrogate them. Me, why me? That's an order and orders are not to be discussed, Agent Toledo, get them for tomorrow because no doubt they're celebrating now, they're always celebrating. You're leaving the worst to me, will you go to Canizales' funeral? They ordered me not to.

Then he called Dr Parra. Is there something new? No, I just wanted to thank you. It's nice to hear that. I got buried in work and last night I slept pretty well. Just don't get too drunk because it'll go crosswise with your pills. So why do you drink so much? I'm the doctor here and don't you forget it. Alright, if I fall off the rails I'll look for you. For the time being continue using the tranquiliser I prescribed and stand firm, you are a prisoner of yourself and it should be the other way around. They hung up. He fought back a sudden memory and once it was dark he decided to return to the scene of the crime.

Two officers on guard in a patrol car greeted him.

They killed him at night, I want to see what it looks like in the dark. In he went. He saw the light switch glowing but did not turn it on. He stood still in the living room, allowing his senses to take the measure of the place. Darkness. He walked slowly down the hall, sniffing, imagining, listening. He pushed the door of the study with his foot and turned on the light: everything in order. Thick-spined books on a set of shelves. A desk with its high-backed chair. Books on the surface. A new computer boxed up in a corner. Pistachio green carpet. Laura was right about that: he was a serious fellow, if the tidiness was anything to go by. He stood still for a moment then retraced his steps. The guest room smelled stuffy. Nothing there to stimulate him. The door to Canizales' bedroom was open. He turned on the light. The fragrance. That fragrance, which in the morning had licked at his brain, again ravaged his senses, though now it was fainter. The sheets on the easy chair. He sniffed them without touching, nodded. Behind the door he found a wastebasket with a Kleenex, he picked it up with the end of his pistol. It smelled the same as the sheets but stronger. He pulled a plastic bag out of his jacket pocket and dropped the Kleenex inside. As I always say: every place is one big word and a lot of small ones, he sniffed the barrel of his weapon, the key is in the small ones. He imagined the man seated across from his victim, Canizales surprised by that redolent presence in the easy chair or on the bed. Maybe he was watching television. Did he like Channel 22? He saw him on his feet begging not to be killed, then the murderer laying him down. Why did he mess up the sheets? Could it be he was sleeping? And suppose they were more than one?

He turned out the light.

He experienced the peace of the defeated and left.

At home he watched television until midnight, took the tranquiliser, and slept fitfully. He awoke with the image of Bardominos the priest hounding his eyes. Fucking life.

Ten

That morning the kid with the bike attended the funeral of Bruno Canizales. He drove the thirty-six kilometres from Culiacán to Navolato in a green pickup his brother-in-law lent him. His two-wheeler stayed in the parking lot of the company where the brother-in-law was the manager. And there he was, standing beside Dania Estrada and Laura Frías, listening to the wails and eyeing the signs of grief. No-one knows what he's got till it's gone, he thought just to think it. The kid was thin, strong, he wore Levi's and a black T-shirt with a picture of Robbie Williams. Engineer Canizales chose not to speak, in his place his son thanked the mourners for their solidarity and their presence. Clear as a cloud. The kid with the bike listened attentively. He watched people from the summits of politics and agriculture gathered around the parents at the pink marble family crypt. A man in a sombrero offered him tequila and he drank a long guzzle straight from the bottle. The girls said they did not drink. The members of the U.S.B. wore white and their svelte appearance contrasted with that of the people from the countryside. The place was filled with flowers to help the soul of the deceased find its way. Figueroa and Dr Ripalda, near the open casket, mumbled a prayer. Figueroa kept his eyes on the heavens, avoiding the cadaver, which the relatives were viewing for the last time.

The interloper saw that the hated Bruno Canizales was indeed truly dead. You moved on, asshole, and for sure these stupid girls are crying because you dumped them too, dude. As far as I'm concerned she killed him, said Laura Frías, who undoubtedly needed to let that out, I keep turning things over and over and I just don't see anyone else, Paola made good on her threat. The police will investigate and justice will be done, Dania reassured her, in any case he is already judged in the eyes of God. The kid with the bike knew what they were talking about, he gave them a disparaging glance and walked away: My queen offed the jerk? stupid old women, they talk just because they have mouths, they'll get what they deserve for making false accusations; what I still can't figure is why you sacrificed yourself for a guy who put you down every chance he got, he didn't deserve you, I mean, did you never see the way he carried on with these chicks? so why?

As my grandfather used to say, women were not born to be understood by dummies like me.

He left the cemetery, the parking lot swollen with official cars and powerful people. Paola's funeral in Culiacán was three hours off. He'd have plenty of time for a ceviche in Altata and still make the Mass at the funeral home. I'm your most stricken widower, my queen, the most afflicted; the one who doesn't know what to do. I'd like to take you up on what you said you saw in that French movie, when the guy's sweetheart dies and he tells another babe: what do you say, kid, shall we? Here's my proposal: as an homage to the guy that's gone, we do it like those nutty missionaries. But I've got the world upside down, my queen, of course I'm no good even for that.

Eleven

Mendieta parked in the street and walked across to Headquarters. Commander Moisés Pineda was exiting the parking lot in a red Lamborghini, the latest model. The detective spotted him, what is that idiot doing here? and he gave a perfunctory wave. The other rolled down his window: How are you, Lefty, what a sight, give me your sister and I'll set you right. He did not like that stupid saying one bit. I'm fine, captain, what's up? Just taking this new baby for a test drive, guess who gave it to me? Pineda loved to try his patience. Nobody, you bought it with your savings. The commander caught the irony, he smiled and winked: We should have a few beers, Lefty, you and I have a lot in common, things we could both profit from, are you ready for some breakfast? He thought: You are a dumb-ass if you think I'd let myself be seen with you, they had entered the police academy at the same time, then each had chosen his own turf. Good idea, Pineda, but it'll have to be some other day, we're busy as can be with the Canizales case. I'll take that as a promise, Briseño isn't in yet, he must be cooking with his old lady, tell him to expect my call; by the way, thanks for yesterday's gangsta-wrap, it turned out to be a lot more lucrative than expected. You know we are here to serve you, captain. They said goodbye.

Mendieta walked towards the building. Robles, a young officer, was covering reception. Is Ortega in? No, sir, but I'll tell you who is, your partner, what a beauty, isn't she? Would you vote for her for Mazatlán carnival queen? I'd even collect donations if she liked, they smiled. The duty officer had *El Debate* on the desk, open to the crime section, at the top they had a big picture of the Piggyback gangsta-wrap. Do they identify him? No. Mendieta was thinking if Pineda knew who it was he would not care to say, especially if it had turned him a profit.

In the cubicle Zelda Toledo was trying to get Mariana Kelly or Marcelo Valdés to take her call. Good morning, he saw the forensic report on the desk, is there anything in Montaño's report we don't already know? Nothing, except that he died at about 4.30 a.m. from a silver bullet and that I'm invited out to dinner tonight, Mendieta smiled, and you know who is going to dinner with him, boss? his grandmother. Does he have one? That's his problem, tell me something, what nut uses silver bullets these days? Vampire hunters, did you watch any of those movies? Two, and I nearly fell asleep from boredom; listen, these people don't want to take my call. He put the bag with the Kleenex on the desk, do we have their addresses? She nodded, will you come with me? As your driver, but first let me make a call, from the desk drawer he pulled out a worn appointment book. What's that Kleenex? I want to identify the fragrance I found at Canizales' house. You went back? Last night, here it is. He dialled, got a hello, and said: So, do you know what I'm eating for breakfast? a dozen quail eggs poached in cranberry sauce, orange juice with nopales, and a macchiato. Well, I'm having lobster salad on rye smeared with tomato sauce and a double cappuccino. L.H. was a master perfume maker who had tired of mixing essential oils and now worked once in a while for the Los Angeles police, as well as for the occasional Mexican friend. They had met at a course in Tijuana, L.H. passing on a couple of useful things in an otherwise tedious talk at Police Headquarters, plus an infinity of secrets the four subsequent nights in several bars across the city. That means you're in heaven. Lefty, my dear friend, what can I do for you. I've got a Kleenex that smells like nirvana, I'm going to send it to you. To the P.O. box I gave you, please. They exchanged a few more pleasantries and hung up.

Agent Toledo, whenever you say.

Zelda opened a drawer in her desk: Boss, I've got the list of calls. Anything new? I think so, she called him eight times between 2.14 and 5.47 a.m. but he didn't answer any of them, they turn up as missed calls on the other end; he made one to Navolato, to his parents' number at 10.13 Thursday night and one before that at 6.05 p.m. to Mazatlán to the Hotel La Siesta; since he died at about 4.30 in the morning it couldn't be Paola; Frank Aldana the dancer is staying at La Siesta, she fell silent. Zelda, have you ever seen an angry tiger put to sleep? What's that about? About us going to find Yoonohoo Valdés. Maybe he's out of the country or in Los Cabos. Did they tell you that? No, but it's Saturday, I don't think those people stay in the city over the weekend. Come on, you don't really believe they work nine to five like the English?

They found Marcelo Valdés' mansion in Colinas de San Miguel, partway up a mountain. It was immense, light green with gilded aluminium doors, and protected by a five-metre-high wall with two turrets clad in purple and yellow ceramic tiles. They knocked. A young man, staring intently with pale eyes, opened the door and waited for the visitors to say something. Zelda Toledo spoke up: We are from Santiago de los Caballeros, we've come to ask a favour of

Don Marcelo. The young man requested instructions by cell phone, Mendieta spotted a camera above the door and turned towards the street, the young man put away the telephone, pulled out an A.K. from somewhere, and holding it in plain view said: The boss doesn't see garbage. He had turned to stone. He doesn't? Lefty said, his face suddenly contorted, but he's the dumpster himself. The sentry raised the rifle, they heard running boots approaching, soon they had three guards standing before them preparing to shoot. Zelda pushed him towards the street: Let's go, boss, you don't want one of these animals filling you full of holes. You're leaving, Lefty Mendieta, without even saying hello? The Gringo stepped forward with an aggressive grin: Put those down, boys, these people are not from Santiago, but they come in peace. Well, I wouldn't want to leave without congratulating you, your security squad is spectacular. My man Lefty, whenever it can be of use to you, it's yours; the boss would be delighted to see you, but he's not in, can I help out with anything? Just one small thing, Gringo, I'd like him to recommend a supplier of silver bullets. They glared at each other, on the boil, the Gringo's smile broad and menacing. Are you planning to put away a werewolf or what? No, they raised my budget at Headquarters and we thought we'd add a touch of class. I'll ask him when he gets in and I'll give you a call, have you got the same number? I hope you haven't forgotten it. What is well learned is never forgotten. I know you threatened Bruno Canizales over his relationship with Samantha, what time of day did you kill him? Doesn't Ortega work with you anymore? he was smiling again, he'll know exactly when, you're peeing outside the bowl, Lefty, I heard he died in bed from a single shot to the head, you know that isn't our style. Tell your boss we'll be back. Come back on Monday if you'd like to tell him yourself.

They got into the Jetta and drove off in silence. When they passed La Lomita, the detective opened his mouth: They say eating is therapeutic, Zelda looked at him surprised, I'll buy you an aguachile.

They went to Roberto's stand next to the Arts Council and set themselves down on the sidewalk in folding chairs with the Modelo brewery logo, amid truck exhaust and rushing pedestrians. Frank Aldana is in Mazatlán, we should bring him in, she said, homosexual romances are passionate and cruel. We will, I don't want to ask the Mazatlecos to do it for us, they might lock him away for the rest of his days, I have a friend over there who could lend us a hand. Could they bring him to us? No, my dear, you will go and get him. Me? boss, please, it had better be soon, next Saturday is Rodo's birthday and I want to spend it with him, don't be bad. You'll be back by then. She looked at him with her big eyes: That's why you took me out for seafood, right? to twist my arm. How could you think such a thing. He's my boyfriend, couldn't it be after his birthday? the guy is taking a course with Delfos, the dance company, I phoned the artistic director, she says he'll be there for several days. What, do you expect him to come back on his own? No, I didn't say that, do I have to bring him in or just interrogate him? O.K., stop whining, I'll go with you, we'll leave early Monday. Why do you do this to me? For police we're such complainers, aren't we, nothing makes us happy. Zelda asked for another hibiscus drink. Did you reach the parents? Nobody answered. Briseño doesn't want us bothering them, so let's pay them a visit this afternoon. Do I have

59

to go with you? No. Boss, it's just that Rodo wants to go to a movie.

Cavalry charge. It was Laura. Do you know that Paola Rodríguez is dead? Oh, yeah? when did you find out? I just heard, we're in Navolato, leaving the cemetery. What did they tell you? That she committed suicide. Oh. Listen, as far as I'm concerned she was the one who killed Bruno, she did it for revenge and to make good on her threat; I heard the wake is being held at the San Chelín on Zapata, in case you want to drop by. Are you going? Absolutely not. What's the atmosphere like over there? It's full of politicians and beautiful people. So it smells good. More or less. What about Engineer Canizales? Prim and proper. Alright, thanks for letting me know.

Truly, that lawyer had the heart of a playboy.

How long has the dancer been at that course? A week. Well, lucky for him he has the alibi of his life. You know what I think, only the narcos could use silver bullets, if they put diamonds in their teeth and wear all that outlandish bling, why wouldn't they use silver bullets? Keep on like that and soon the Russians really will come for you. Is that good or bad? The detective looked at her, he liked her so he decided not to leave her with the old joke. While he finished his shrimp and drank the spicy broth he explained a few things about being a detective.

She listened attentively. Why wasn't he married? What should she make of the rumours she heard sometimes at Headquarters?

Mariana Kelly lived on Valadés Parkway in a modern apartment building. This time Mendieta did not want to get out of the car. Five minutes later, Toledo returned with the news that she was not at home. According to the doorman, a man of fifty or so, she usually spent weekends in Altata with her dog and with Señora Valdés and her son.

What shall we do? Get the telephone number.

At Headquarters they found a copy of *News from the Empire* by Fernando del Paso with a note from Guillermo Ortega: "Jack the Ripper". He had heard a lot about the book so he decided to take it home. Zelda found the number in the directory and called. The caretaker answered, they were not there, nor were they coming. Mendieta knew he should not hold her up, that she had a date with her boyfriend, yet he made her suffer right up to the moment he left for Navolato.

Twelve

The kid with the bike stamped into the room where the wake for Paola Rodríguez was under way. Aroma of roses. People everywhere. Packed in. His gang was by the entrance, for whatever might be needed. The father was beside the coffin, once in a while he moved his head and a tear ran down his cheek. The mother sat in the front row, lifeless. Utterly lifeless. Flower wreaths beribboned with the names of the donors overflowed the usual space. Everyone was talking. In one corner Beatriz's friends commiserated with her about Jesús González Dávila's play "My Dearest Girl" and the pitiful audiences it was attracting: Being the best dramatist in Mexico isn't enough, so what that he's a human rights advocate, people don't know what that means. All the effort we put into acting is useless too, we live in one big dusty hovel. He positioned himself in the furthest corner and observed the crowd, most of them friends of the family because she was never very outgoing. Dante and his buddies from the university were drinking brandy, talking, one of them was telling jokes. Only her father and I loved her, the kid thought, me more than him, more than all of them, more than I love myself. Too bad the last cannot be first.

I said no, I don't want sex, I don't want anything. Girl, what's wrong, don't you see the way I am? Quit bugging me, and stop slobbering, you don't know how to kiss, you just drool all over me, you pig, you savage, don't touch my bra, no! leave me alone, Zeke, please, I'm at the end of my rope. I love you Paola, I'm crazy about you, I've got to have you, I want to be the love of your life. Not today, not now, stop, I couldn't care less what you want from me, sweet fuck all; less than sweet fuck all.

Beatriz sat down beside him. Babe, he said, you must be happy, there's one thing going round and round in my head, sometimes I think you're the one who sent her packing. Oh no, she did it on her very own, and now you've run out of excuses, my king. I may not have any but I need time. What for? everything is crystal clear. If I say I need it, I need it babe, don't push me. As long as it's not too much time, oh, and I don't want to see you anywhere near that coffin, no long goodbyes, and don't you dare volunteer to be a pall-bearer. You are such a bitch, you don't even try to hide it. You stink of fish, where did you have lunch?

She stood up quickly to receive the condolences of several women from the neighbourhood and the director of the play, who guided her away, his arm around her waist.

The kid with the bike blinked: I want to make you mine, Zeke, you are the toughest dude in the hood and the one I want to do it with, they were in the living room of her house. Beatriz shed her blouse and undid her pants. Forget it, babe, put that shit back on, he threw the blouse at her. I thought of everything except you saying no. I don't care what you thought, I'm in love with your sister, and I'm in it down to my little fingers, so I can't fall for anyone else or satisfy your desires. It also never occurred to me you were a faggot. Well, yeah, maybe I am, what of it.

He got to his feet. The funeral home staff were rolling the open casket into the chapel for the ceremony. People began drifting over. The mother was sobbing. There's nothing in life I hate more than being a fucking dunce, the kid lamented. I never understood you and even less now. What is it, babe, why did you kill yourself? I never saw you lacking for a thing. It's true: there is nothing I hate more.

Thirteen

A little after five in the afternoon, Mendieta arrived at the Canizales compound on the outskirts of Navolato, a prosperous, hot, humid town founded by commercial farmers. A strong breeze made the leaves flutter. The drivers of several government cars were making small talk, all smiles. They were listening to northern corridos with the volume low. Immense fruit trees easily reached over the wall surrounding the orchard. He identified himself to the man at the gate who led him to a little room that smelled of apple-scented air freshener. A television had the ball game on: Vinicio Castilla at bat. Through a small window he could see part of a two-storey, ochre-yellow house full of arches and greenery, mostly ferns and golden chains. In the garden, avocado, mango, and orange trees, an arbour where men in sombreros were conversing around a flask of cane liquor.

Nicolás Beltrán, the family lawyer, meticulously shaven and dressed in a black suit, came to tell him the engineer could not see him, that he hoped he would please understand. I do understand, and that's why I only want to ask him one question. Any interruption would be uncalled for, Señor Mendieta, he is exhausted and of course very upset. Just the one and I won't bother him again. Look, I spoke with Commander Briseño and he agreed the engineer would not be inconvenienced, however I can see that there are broken links in the chain of command, I shall have to call the district attorney's office. Mendieta felt such a deep weariness at the mention of his higher-ups, it drained the blood from his face and made him want nothing more than to behave himself, so he took the emissary by the lapels, lifted him off the ground, and threw him against the wall: Listen asshole, take me to your boss right this minute or I'll charge you with obstructing the investigation and throw you in the slammer for a week, and then you can tell me how you'll fix things to get yourself out. The lawyer was petrified, his mouth agape. Let's go, the detective ordered while he smoothed a wrinkle in his coat and pushed the man towards the door. The lawyer turned to him and poked a finger into his chest. I don't want you to leave, Mendieta, without knowing that you just earned yourself an enemy. You? suck my dick, I just took a look at your file and it's this thick. He spun him around and gave him a shove.

The engineer was enjoying the company of friends from government and business. They were drinking hard, smoking cigars. The lawyer gave him the word and he threw a glare at the detective, who held his gaze just to see how it felt to confront a potentate, then came over to greet him with the cordiality of a politician: Come with me in here. People were talking in little groups, he could see the brother and his friends making a few girls smile; among the friends, one that was elegantly dressed caught his eye, where have I seen him before? They sat down in an office big enough to hold eight of the detective's little cubicle.

Tell me what makes you so anxious to see me. Your son was murdered with a silver bullet by someone who knew him; Engineer Canizales, you are a very important man with numerous friends and enemies, have you received any threats? None whatsoever, and there was sufficient distance between myself and my son that my enemies would take that into account, I know he was a great lawyer, but it has been more than four years since we last spoke, don't ask me why; I will ask the district attorney to suspend the investigation and you will be able to move on to another case; I am not interested in knowing the identity or the fate of my son's murderer, pause, firm gesture, icy glower, so don't waste your time, I know what country I live in and what can be avoided, if you will excuse me I must return to my friends, he stood up. Do you know why the D.A.'s office already called asking for the same thing? Impasse during which no-one dares touch a thing. Aha, like Bruno used to say when he was little: Do you swear? My brother was the same way, yes, I swear. Detective, I have serious differences with the district attorney, if he ordered the investigation suspended then I will make sure it continues right to the end, even though the results are still immaterial to me. O.K., I trust you will treat this delicately with District Attorney Bracamontes. Carry on, detective, I will call for an update, any other questions? What fragrance is this? Canizales started for the door. I have no idea. Neither did the detective, rumours are flying that your party is going to make a shift and the lucky one will be you. I cannot speak to what has not occurred. What I meant was that you can count on my vote. Thank you. Did Bruno have a room here? No, he rarely stayed here and when he did he slept in his brother's room. The narcos had your son in their sights, he was threatened by Marcelo Valdés, did you know that? No, and seriously, detective, the last thing I want is for this to snowball, especially if those people are involved. Mendieta looked at him: Thank you, engineer, don't forget that you can count on my vote and the votes of my family.

Under the arbour no-one was speaking. Wasps flitted from one sombrero to another. A woman dressed in black asked him to approach. Thin. Pale as death. Hands transparent. Are you from the police? Edgar Mendieta of the State Ministerial Police, at your service. I am Bruno's mother, I don't know how to prove it, but I am certain he had him killed, he's a bastard, a monster who will burn in hell. Her mouth was twisted with hatred. What makes you think it was him? Because he has never had any scruples and he did not approve of my boy's lifestyle; his ambition is boundless, do you know who he has brought into his circle? the scum of his party, she looked at him, her eyes dry. On Thursday night, did your son speak with you after ten o'clock? He called from Mazatlán; he was happy, he told me he was by the sea. Beltrán came hurrying over, followed by two nurses: Enough, Mendieta, you'll see what you'll get for sticking your nose in where it doesn't belong; señora, you should rest. The nurses took charge of the woman, who did not say a word. Beltrán faced the detective: You can scram. I could also stay and have a drink with these people. You're a dumbass, he said, heading off as quickly as he had come. Mendieta smiled happily.

"Two gangsta-wraps, each with its coup de grâce, were found in a rural area along the highway to Imala; Commander Moisés Pineda, chief of the Anti-Narcotics Unit of the Federal Preventive Police, went in person to the scene of the crime and declared that they are hot on the trail of the murderers and will spare no effort to put them behind bars. On another matter, little news in the case of Attorney Bruno Canizales, murdered two days ago at his home in Guadalupe neighbourhood; Commander Omar Briseño reported to this station that the perpetrators of the crime will soon be caught and there will be no funny business. The investigation is being led by Detective Edgar 'Lefty' Mendieta, one of the most prestigious and incorruptible members of the force, and results are expected soon. For 'Eyes on the Night' weekend edition, this is Daniel Quiroz reporting."

He parked his car at El Quijote. You are two bricks short of a load, fucking Quiroz, you haven't a clue, and when you do, you shut your trap, and shutting up is a priceless virtue if you live in hell and have to speak with the devil.

He sat near the bar, far from the stage where a dark-skinned girl was dancing to Barry White's "Under the Influence of Love". The place was a sound box. They sent a beer over and a double tequila, which he downed quickly. He was thirsty. They served him again. The waiter, a homosexual known as Curlygirl, was from the Col Pop and he held Lefty in high regard: he had known his mother, whom he referred to as a stern but understanding woman. At the next table over, a man was yammering at a beer that had grown warm. No-one paid any attention to him. My God has eyes and nothing escapes him, my God has ears and hears all, my God has skin and feels everything; He shall soon be here to set things straight and the impious shall pay: all the criminals with starched collars, the corrupt judges, the people who set the price of coffee and tobacco, all of them will pay. He really needs his snort, Curlygirl murmured, while serving the detective his third drink. Well, get it for him and you'll have your ticket to heaven assured. If only your mother could hear you, may God hold her close, so little time left and you giving me advice. He saw coming through the door the cheerleader for the Tomateros who had gone to bed with the forensic doctor, accompanied by two girlfriends and a transvestite. All three girls were attractive, lithe, fit, long hair full of highlights and coloured strands, pierced belly buttons on view; and the tranny was not about to be left behind. Just look at that quartet, a fascinated Curlygirl exclaimed, no doubt swept away by some recollection because right away he said: What times those were. Who is he? He's one of the Valenzuelas, Lefty. You don't say, the son of Yoonohoo Valenzuela? No more, no less. Would he have known Bruno Canizales? he wondered and grew thoughtful, noticing how they drew the attention of the crowd, which sent a steady stream of drinks their way. The girls were happy, they had more admirers than the dancers, who were certainly awful that night, same as the comic. The one on stage at the moment had her top off to dance a polka, but not even that made the crowd look up. Mendieta entered an easy state of drunkenness, controlled drunkenness, in which he never allowed himself to remember anything except the fact that he had to save his own skin. The last time he let himself wallow in memories, he did not go to work for a week and it took Ortega and Montaño's determined efforts to raise him from prostration. Dr Parra, I hope not to see you for a long time, my friend; I promise I will never again be weak and if I feel any commotion I'll cut off my balls. Goga: the name surfaced, and with it a gorgeous face, a smile, a way of walking, and he drank. Goga, why don't you come and pick up the pieces? they're scattered in the sewers, chewed on by the rats. Shaking his head, Curlygirl watched him: Edgar, drop all that, my son, the world is full of women. Don't say that, bro, don't say it and don't believe I'm not frightened by the fact that all those women come down to one. It's love, my son, and there is but one way out; to our eternal disgrace, it's a fatal trap, remember what happened to me with my lieutenant colonel; you've got to just leave it, there's no other way, sweetie, what, aren't you a man? Mendieta quickly drained his beer and the tequila. The waiter shook his head hopelessly. The addicted believer abandoned his table; his supplier had not turned up, so he headed off to another dive.

Another beer, then he decided it was time to leave. What would become of man without the night? In the car he swallowed a Ranisen and chewed a Pepto for heartburn. He turned on the stereo and the Stones' version of "Like a Rolling Stone" kicked off, which he found both subtle and captivating. Their satanic majesties in style, as loud as could be. He recalled that *Milenio Diario* had published a list of covers of Stones tunes, which he was sure was incomplete. It did not even have Joe Cocker's "A Little Help from My Friends", which is a monument, or Janis' "To Love Somebody", or "Proud Mary" by Tina Turner. Two black Hummers were double-parked across from the bar. Well now, for whom do the bells toll? Maybe they went in to celebrate and I've just got a suspicious mind. Should he snoop around or hold his curiosity in check? He preferred to keep his distance from the narcos for two reasons: one, his best friend had been artfully peppered with bullets simply for insisting on his fee for taking a suitcase of cocaine to Ciudad Juárez, and that came after they had raped his girlfriend and tortured him. They had gone to school together and it left a mark that could not be erased. And two, when he was already in the police they tried to take him out twice: once in a memorable gunfight where the car in which he took cover caught fire, and the other when they planted twenty-seven kilos of Novocain on him so he would lose his job. I slipped free both times, he thought, weary of it all. That very day he resigned from Narcotics and, according to those in the know, from the easy, expedited road to riches.

Eight minutes later, he saw them come out with the cheerleaders and the tranny, get into their vehicles, and peel away, burning rubber.

Once the song ended, he started the Jetta; like a blessing, the way Goga walked to the bathroom filled his mind, but only for an instant. Does sashay come from sachet? Then, listening to the Monkees' "A Little Bit Me, a Little Bit You", he drove home to the Col Pop.

Fourteen

It was getting dark. In a small room overlooking the back garden, Marcelo Valdés and his wife were talking. They were drinking fruit-flavoured chamomile tea. Three bodyguards were on strict alert. It was your call to settle down here, you said being near your family was what counted. What I really wanted was to get you away from you know who, she gave him a cold look, and if you still have even a drop of shame you won't make me recall that bitch, she was leafing through a fashion magazine. Valdés ignored her and continued: Now you want us to move back to the country, where do you get the idea it's a paradise? My love, you're ill, you've got more commitments than you can possibly keep, and I don't want you to die; I lost my son and I don't want to lose you. We're all born to die. But not at the hands of our enemies or from anger; Dr Elenes says you'd be wise to retire, go back to the country, and live in peace, you can't handle the stress the way you could before, things are getting tougher every day, and up there we have Sky, the plane, enough food for a year; all that's missing is us. They fell silent, Valdés noticed the darkness growing denser, though they remained in the shadows, the lights in the garden came on. I have created an empire that will die with me, he moaned as if to himself, but his wife responded: I don't think Samantha would agree, don't you see how upset she is about your illness? Look, I think about her a lot, maybe too much, and it worries me that she still gets those teenage tantrums. Well, even with all that, she is a far sight better than the good-for-nothings who came to visit you today. Two of his sons from other women had come to the house at noon to see about his condition, both were doctors, specialists, but the wife did not let them examine him, claiming Dr Elenes was jealous about his patients. Neither of them is interested in this business, he sidestepped, serving himself more tea. I wouldn't be so sure. They have their hospital, and it's fully accredited, by the way. But they are human, and if they're human they are ambitious and they aren't going to just take things lying down, which is why you had better start thinking about Samantha, she grew up with you and you know everything about her, the others, well, who knows what tricks they might have up their sleeves. Again, they fell silent.

Someone turned on the house lights. They heard a car come in. It was Samantha's Hummer. She and Mariana got out, carrying the sleeping child; the señora called them over and took charge of the little boy, who continued sleeping, undisturbed. What are you up to, are you getting romantic? Yeah right, your father won't try to lasso me, he's a bore. Is that true, Pa, aren't you the big macho? Mariana went for cold drinks. It's just that she doesn't know how to dance. What do you mean, I'd even do a flamenco for you if I got the chance. I mean on horseback. Not even if I were nuts. Don't say no, Ma, I'll help you, I'll hold the reins so you can mount. If we can dance on the floor, why do we have to dance in the air? The old guy wants to cut loose, Mama, you have to give him a chance. Mariana came back with two glasses of Coke. They continued talking until the girls departed. Valdés still felt uncomfortable, something told him things were not right. That policeman, Mendieta, he was begging to be taught a lesson, how could it have occurred to him to bother him at home, was it not enough that he paid off the top brass to leave him in peace? By the time he went to bed, after a supper of toast and yogurt, he had made up his mind.

Fifteen

On Sunday he awoke with the image of the priest Bardominos in his thoughts. He got up feeling tired, he had slept with the television on, and feeling troubled that he could not wipe such a hurtful image from his memory. He dragged up Parra's words: Seek out intellectual enjoyment, mental exercises that give you pleasure, like learning something new, works of art, books, concerts, crossword puzzles; force yourself, most of our intelligence springs from our emotions and you cannot spend your whole life carrying around that open wound, it's really important for you to fall in love.

He made a Nescafé and picked up the copy of the novel *News from the Empire* that Ortega had left him. Paola Rodríguez's name was on the flyleaf. "I am Marie Charlotte of Belgium, Empress of Mexico and of America. I am Marie Charlotte Amélie, cousin of the Queen of England, Grand Magister of the cross of Saint Charles, and Vicereine of the Lombardo-Veneto Provinces, which Austria's clemency and mercy has subsumed under the two-headed eagle of the House of Habsburgs."

Well now, he chuckled, if I remember correctly this woman went insane. Did Paola admire her? Was Bruno her Maximilian? Nobles who kill each other with silver bullets but would never desecrate the bodies, high-class people who demonstrate their decorum in their most villainous acts. Not bad; however, the weapons are not the same and suppose Ortega was wrong? Impossible.

He continued reading. The further into the novel he got, the more absorbed he became and that offered a break from his professional ruminations. At eleven the landline rang.

Hello. Edgar Mendieta? Yes. This is Samantha Valdés, I heard you were looking for me and I figured I'd call you first, where can we see each other in an hour?

What, now the ducks shoot at the hawks?

They shook hands.

Samantha was tall, perfect measurements if a bit too large at the hips; rumour had it she had spent a fortune on plastic surgeons, but not even the Brazilians had managed to get it right. Red tresses, thin lips, green eyes, nails painted purple; her soft perfume had not been floating in Canizales' room, at least not the scent she had on at the moment. She wore black and had arrived in a green Hummer, which the detective spied through the window. An H3. She parked it next to the botanical gardens named for Carlos Murillo Depraect. A black pickup with tinted windows carrying the bodyguards she preferred to keep out of her sight had pulled up a few metres behind her.

She was a strong-willed woman who did not like to waste time: What's bothering you, Lefty Mendieta? Did his voice crack? no, were his palms sweaty? not a chance, did he lower his eyes? not even in your dreams. The detective liked the way she used the familiar *tú*, the way she took a sip of the coffee he had in front of him and made fun of the dishwater people drank in every government office. Canizales was killed with a silver bullet, do you know anyone who uses them? Lots, though only two of them live here, and, if you don't mind me saying, they would be the last people interested in someone like Bruno, they're people of a certain stature. People of a certain stature also get spattered with blood. What do you know? Oh, you learn a few things being a policeman, despite what you may have been told. People like you don't reach those heights, understand? she gave him a cold, irritated smile. Mendieta chose not to pursue the matter.

He asked for another espresso, she for a Frappuccino. The place was overflowing with chattering women. During the week they left their children at school and congregated here until classes let out: they gossiped about diets, fashion, diseases, useless husbands, high-spirited secretaries. On Sundays many of them continued the gabfest while their husbands watched soccer or got drunk with their friends.

I sought you out for two reasons, Mendieta: first, respect my father, asshole; he is one of the most important men in this country; the president, his ministers, and every brown-noser around them salutes him, if it weren't for him millions of people would be unemployed and dying of hunger, who are you to harass him at home? a worthless, starving policeman; second, do not bother Mariana Kelly, do you hear me? she had nothing to do with that murder, but she's anxious, she once threatened him in public so she's afraid of being interrogated. What are you worried about? your daddy will fix everything in the time it takes to say amen. I don't want you to mix my father up in this, jerk-off, your disdain I understand, but I don't give a fuck, to each his own and don't think for a minute I sought you out for your pretty face, I'll pay you for the favour. You can take your money and your father's money and shove it up your ass and, stay where you are, girlie, hold it right there, because I don't have time for cheap theatrics. Red-lipped smile, a woman accustomed to difficult moments: Say whatever you like, you'll always be a piece of shit. Mendieta's face grew hard: I'm not playing, Samantha Valdés, and now that we're into it, I hope you'll answer a few questions. I'll answer whatever you want as long as you do the same, and don't make me suspicious, asshole, because I'll be after you wherever you go, she paused, her features like stone. He was going to reply but decided to change the subject. Tell me about your relationship with Bruno Canizales. I liked how he did it with me, he drove me wild, that man had a feeling for the body, for sexual sensations, for time, for smell, he made everyone else look like a moron; I'd give him a ten and even an eleven if that's allowed; and then my son became really attached to him, he even took him to the park and he had the patience his father never had, end of story. I'll pay for your Frappu if you'll tell me where you were last Thursday night. At home, Friday was the final episode of "To Die on Your Breast" and I wasn't going to miss the one before it for anything in the world. At last, the detective thought, someone who does not watch Channel 22. How did you learn about Bruno Canizales' death? From the newspaper, so would he take her off the list? No, first he needed to learn a couple of things: Did you know Paola Rodríguez? Of course, a goddamn witch who kept getting in Bruno's way, the idiot freaked out when I took her down a few pegs, I sent over a couple of thugs to shake her up a bit and it worked like a charm, people have such bad manners, why don't they leave you in peace? What makes you think Mariana had nothing to do with it? She doesn't go to such extremes, she's really a "live and let live" girl, and besides she wouldn't lie to me. You are her goddess. Something like that, she believes they're going to come for her sooner or later and she's terrified, I told her the Mexican police are useless, that my dad has them all bought and paid for, we even made a couple of calls when we knew they were looking for her, but she's convinced they're going to put the squeeze on her and she doesn't want trouble; the district attorney gave us your boss' telephone and he gave us yours; we calculated your price more or less, would you prefer Madrid, Paris, New York, or cash, I'm talking about two weeks all inclusive, and, of course, accompanied by whomever you choose, since we've heard the rumours about you, she smiled knowingly. I find your pragmatism charming, who are the ones who use silver bullets? I'm not going to tell you, Bruno didn't even register in their world and I don't believe those people would shoot at anyone; stop playing the fool, you only live once and you ought to live it. Thank you for the advice. So? she pulled a manila envelope out of her bag and laid it in front of him. Mendieta spied Rudy Jiménez by the cash register and waved to him, the café's owner winked and smiled. Tell Mariana Kelly if she thinks it's going to happen, it will, and tell her to expect me, I'll be by for her tomorrow, same story with your father. You are a son of a bitch, Mendieta, and you know what, you are going to regret it, sharp breath in, my father I don't worry about, he can take care of himself, I'd like to see you try to lay a finger on Mariana so you'll finally learn who you are dealing with, asshole. She picked up the envelope, stood up, dumped over the rest of her coffee and stalked off. O.K.

Rudy quickly wiped the table with a cloth. No question about it, you are a man of fixed tastes, detective, you like them wild. I've got to be consistent in something, don't you think? You like the debauched life, listen, if you get your appetite back, my wife just returned from Berlin and she brought back a ham that'll make you die of natural causes, would you care to try some? Later, I've got to go to Headquarters. Don't dismiss it like that, life comes down to good meals and knowing how to get through the times in between. Not now, but if you don't leave me any I'll set the Health Department on you. A nice-looking thin man with a moustache approached. Do you know Ferocious Rendón? Rudy had called him over. I've not had the pleasure, they shook hands. I'll leave you, Jiménez went back to his office. Detective, you studied literature, right? Yes, but I wouldn't do it again. I remember seeing you at the university, you were always late to class and you yawned the whole time. Ah, you teach Hispanic-American literature, but I never had you. No, you took it with Liz. Short and chubby, right. Rudy tells me you're a detective and you hate detective novels. There's something to that. But I didn't ask him to introduce us for that reason; I have a problem, I don't know if you can help. Try me. A month ago my car was stolen, I reported it to the insurance company, and the only thing they've done is give me the runaround, I probably spent more money chasing after the things they want than I should have; tell me if there is any way I can oblige them to pay me or failing that for the police to find the car, the fact is I'm fed up with all the back and forth. I'm in Homicide, professor, go to Headquarters and look for Señor Urrea in the Department of Stolen Vehicles, tell him I sent you, see if something can still be done. Rendón thanked him and went back to his table to continue drinking beer.

While he was paying, he thought how great it was that Samantha was bisexual, he did not think there was a man or woman anywhere in the world that could turn her crank. There are women for whom *everything* will never be enough.

Sixteen

The kid with the bike and Beatriz were talking in bed after making love. They were smoking marijuana and drinking cold beers, which they took out of a small green cooler. They were in a motel.

I don't feel right, he muttered after toking on the freshly rolled joint. Well I do, at last I've got that brat off my back; you have no idea what hell it was living with her, she was a like vacuum cleaner sucking up all the affection, all the money, all the ideas, all the opportunities; nothing saw the light in that house unless it fit her atrocious taste; even when she was little she was insufferable and I was the one who had to take care of her because my mother never loved her; I've had to be careful, but these days have been the best days in my life, first because I have you all to myself and second because I don't have to share the house or the hallways with anyone; the other bedroom is for me now, in a few days I'll move over there so you can climb in the window, since you already know the way; I'll hang some heavy drapes to keep out the curious. They smoked, the kid kept his eyes closed. That damn witch turned the pictures around so there would be no witnesses, can you believe it? nothing could be sicker than that; Papa is drinking a bit, but that will pass and then I'll be his princess. The kid recalled: Zeke, turn those pictures, turn them around, you animal! I don't want them to see the way you abuse me and I don't want to be looking at Bruno. You aren't seeing straight, babe, to put it another way, you are absolutely nuts. About you, I'm not going to deny it, I live life fully, the human drama, I swear I finally understand Shakespeare, when are you going to see the play? I already saw it. But when are you going to go again? Too much effort, those friends of yours are pathetic, all of them, and that idiot that kisses you is falling for you, you know? try to make him chill out. That's acted, don't believe it. Well, I don't like it, he grabs you by the ass like he wanted something else and at the funeral parlour I saw him put his arm around your waist. I love it when you get jealous. You're going to love it more if one day I bust that guy's fucking chops. If he stops kissing me will you come and see it? I didn't say that. But I'm asking, you have to do something to forget her, I forgave you for getting involved with her, I haven't told you but I spied on you two a lot, I'd hear you come in, listen to your moans, and I heard how she would put you down, it really bothers me that you're still stuck on her. I could give a fuck, remember you didn't seduce me, you tricked me when you pretended to be her in her bed, so I don't know which of you two is more of a pervert. The bros say you wouldn't hurt a fly, but the fly you should have killed has polluted half the planet and caused three epidemics with thousands of victims. She kissed him happily, having confirmed that every angel is terrifying.

He smoked, passed her the joint. Why this bad vibe? It's not like he was the son of a lowlife, right? Paola had always mocked him, treated him like a loser, she got off making him feel miserable: Don't put your disgusting tongue in my mouth, idiot, you stink, get out of my life, you flea-bitten dog, I don't want to see you ever again, you make me sick.

Whoever does not deserve love deserves nothing.

Let's stop seeing each other, babe. Why? Beatriz brought her face close. Zeke, please don't do this to me, without her everything will be easier, I love you, I'm sick with love for you, dying for you, ready to do anything for you, I bet everything on a glance. You're too much to carry, Betty, and right now I'm weak, I'm frail, I'm really zonked. Don't be so inconsiderate, Zeke, don't be like that. Did I promise you a rose garden? No, but. So? he imagined everything going dark, Paola watching with a knowing look, unsmiling, disapproving; he threw his bottle against the wall: Get over it, babe, your future isn't me. But why stop seeing each other, we could meet once a week, keep our idyll alive, tell me you don't think it's incredible how we do it. He gave her a lightly scornful look: O.K., babe, but only when I ask for it. She kissed him, when will that be? She gave me a book, when I finish reading it. What book? One about a crazy queen, *News from the Empire*, I don't remember the author. Is it short? More or less. That means we'll see each other in a few days, right? When I finish it. I'll be at the window as much as I can, give me a sign. Oh, but if that asshole grabs your ass again you won't ever see me in your shitty life. Oooo, what a tough guy, she smiled. He gave her a fed-up look and sucked on what was left of the joint.

Seventeen

Five in the morning on the bedside clock, eight at night in his prickly unconscious. A cascade of images made him think he had better face the therapist. He would call him as soon as he got back. He went into the bathroom, suppose he called Zelda and they went off right away? They could have breakfast at the Playa or the Shrimp Bucket. He did not think it wise. He looked at his drawn face, his whiskers a bit long, but he did not feel up to shaving. Mondays are like that, a toboggan into the void, a fruit without any juice. He made a Nescafé and tried to think about the case, he went through the pics on his cell phone and the ones Ortega had given him. Neat and tidy everywhere, like nothing had happened to him. Again the memory of that mysterious fragrance came to mind. Paola had probably been there, since it also smelled of her Carolina Herrera; why use a silver bullet? what kind of message was that? for whom? why? does Frank Aldana know how to shoot? if it was him, why a silver bullet?

Valdés and his clan could use silver bullets or even gold if they felt like it, why is Mariana Kelly afraid to talk to the police? We are going to need a search warrant, should I ask Robles to drop by Laura's house? She's in the picture too. Ortega should go along.

And suppose Bruno's mother is right? what could be so serious that a politician would break off his relationship with his son? his bisexuality? Power corrupts, dissolute power corrupts dissolutely. Imagine that. Are you sure, Mr Engineer, sir? isn't he your son? Look, I pay you to kill not to ask questions. Evidently, the world will have to be set straight by the few of us who are not covering up for the powerful.

While he was musing, Trudis, the heavyset middle-aged woman who kept house for him, arrived with an open newspaper in her hands. Good morning, Lefty, guess how many gangsta-wraps turned up today. He did not know. Four, they found them in Lima, Tierra Blanca, La Costerita, and Bacurimí. He wondered if any of them had a silver bullet. You're off in the clouds, Lefty, what's wrong? come on, take heart, have you had any breakfast? I've got no appetite. Again? He said nothing. Do you have to go out early? At 8.20. Then there is time for you to eat something, I'm going to make you some eggs with spring onions and turkey bacon that will wash away your sins. Later. None of this later, I won't let you leave on an empty stomach and don't push me away because soon you'll be thanking me, now go shave, you are a respectable man, I don't want anyone to see you looking like a beggar.

Quarter past nine in the morning. They went through the tollbooth on the Culiacán–Mazatlán highway and stopped to buy coffee at a stand at the side of the road. About twenty metres ahead of them, the Federal Highway Police had set up a roadblock for truckers. They were taking urine samples, and blood too if they thought it necessary, to see how high the men behind the wheel were. Mendieta cheered up as he watched a group of drivers heading for the toilets; others were coming out smiling, obviously in good spirits. One sugar for me and I'll meet you at the car, he told Zelda, and he went into the toilet. A short man was drinking water from a bottle with one hand while with the other he held up several vials filled with yellow liquid.

Hey, my man Shorty, what's up, how's business, two drivers about to purchase their vials looked up, worried. My man Lefty, what a joy for the eyes, he gave him an affectionate hug. Let me finish with these gentlemen and I'll be right with you, the drivers paid for their urine samples and went to do their drug test; he asked another who arrived for the same reason to come back in a minute. Shorty Abitia and he had been friends since childhood. You damn dwarf, I never thought you would do so well. It's the times, Lefty my man, as long as the federal agents are here I'll make enough to bring home the beans, and what about you? on the radio I heard you were caught up in something heavy. Justice never sleeps, my man Shorty, but you know that. Well, if there is anything to be made out of it, keep me in mind, my family will thank you. Alright, clean the wax out of your ears, I want to know who's using silver bullets, 9mm. What luxury, bro, a death like that even I . . . is that how they killed the lawyer? I will expect your call and don't fuck up your kidneys, how many of those are you selling a day? Not many, yesterday I sold fifty-two. Great, now you're going to be set for life. Don't fool yourself, the children are in school and they're a bottomless pit. But it's worth the effort, isn't it? Begoña is already in university. Damn, Shorty, I hope she doesn't turn out like you. Why not? So she doesn't end up a single mom, that's why. May your tongue turn to pork rinds, you'll see how beautiful she'll be wearing white. Keep your ears open and I'll expect to hear from you soon.

When he left the place, seven drivers were in the entranceway, anguish in their faces, while the first one he had seen was in his cab driving off happily towards the city.

In an hour and a half, they had put 180 kilometres of highway behind them and were on the shore drive of the prettiest port on the Pacific.

The sea here is the ultimate muse.

The Municipal School of Dance, where the Delfos Company offered classes, was downtown, next to Ángela Peralta Theatre and across from Machado Square. Claudia Lavista, the group's driving force, greeted them. Mendieta found her attractive, but he made no comment. In her office they let her know they wanted to speak with Frank Aldana. Something bad? Not at all, we just want his assistance.

Seven minutes later, Aldana came in, thirty-two years old, big black eyes, eyebrows like Frida Kahlo's. Visibly nervous when he learned they were from the police. What are you doing here? Zelda began, they had agreed she would do most of the interrogating. I'm in a professional course to perfect my Limón technique for a show, what's up? I'll ask the questions, when was the last time you went to Culiacán? I haven't gone, I came here two weeks ago and I'll be here one more. Who knows you are here? The people from my company and my family. Do you miss the city? I don't have time, the days here are long and exhausting and the teacher is from New York so we can't skip out on anything. How long has it been since you last saw Bruno Canizales? Three months, six days, and about eight hours. Why so precise? I have to keep track, I can't think of any other way to express my longing to see him. Has he called you? No, at least no-one has given me a message at the hotel and I don't have a cell phone. What were you doing Thursday night? I went to sleep, we didn't finish until ten and the call for Friday morning was 9.00 a.m., this interrogation reminds me of the movies, did something happen?

Can any witness confirm you were in at that hour? I'm staying at the Hotel La Siesta, I don't think the management would have noticed, on Friday I had breakfast at eight and by nine I was here, any of my classmates could tell you. If Attorney Canizales died at about 4.30, this bastard could easily have travelled to Culiacán and got back for breakfast; Mendieta was surprised to see how his eyes filled with tears when Zelda told him that Bruno Canizales had been murdered.

Once he had recovered: How did it happen? A bullet to the head. It was that bitch, I'm sure, she was always threatening him, cursing him. Who are you talking about? Paola Rodríguez, an old girlfriend who hated me and hated him, too, a ridiculous, pretentious girl completely full of herself thanks to her beauty and Sor Juana's poetry; she'd bring him thick books supposedly so they could read them together. Like *News from the Empire*? He nodded. Would you testify against her? I'd like to kill the bitch, the envious fucker, since she was incapable of being happy she made sure no-one else was either. Hours later they found her dead at her house. That is just what she always swore, she would kill him and then kill herself, I hope she rots in hell. Then he was sobbing: What do you feel when you fire a gun, I've never done it. If you have no witnesses that you were here Thursday night, you will have to come with us. Take me, nothing matters, I wanted to do this show for him, I'm taking this course for him, everything I wanted to do was for him, even if we hadn't seen each other for a long time he would come to the show and then he'd come to my dressing room to hug me and kiss me and we'd be happy for a few days or a few hours, he was like that and it didn't take much to please me. They fell silent, the man and the woman had also lost people they loved and they understood. We have to go, Mendieta said softly. Aldana stood up, if you'll allow me, I'll get my things.

What do you think, boss? You know, I can't tell when love is mixed up in it, I've never understood lovers who kill each other or prey on each other. Not even when you were in love? Never, and I can't remember the last time I fell in love, he lied, I think it was in kindergarten. In my case, I'd have no idea what sort of mess I'd be in if it weren't for Rodo. I envy you, he lied again, a stable love is the best thing that could happen to anyone. Boss, can I tell you something? at Headquarters that's not what they say about you. What do they say? That you can't shake off an impossible love, that before you were happier, more communicative. Don't pay attention to those assholes, they aren't playing with a full deck. I've got a proposal, boss, let's leave this kid alone, let him live his life, let him stay to take his classes or whatever, why should we make his tragedy worse? Claudia Lavista came in, tall, svelte, white pants, lovely. I'm sorry, I thought you left with Frank. What? They ran outside, in the street the usual throng of pedestrians made it impossible either to see or to run. Sorry, boss, Zelda grunted, I guess this is why we think everyone is guilty even if they seem the opposite. Yup, Frank Aldana just made the mistake of his life, wait until I get my hands on him.

The streets of Mazatlán are narrow; those that do not lead to the sea lead nowhere. Lavista confirmed that Aldana was there Friday at nine the day Canizales died, and that, yes, he had finished the previous day at ten, and she added that he was a very dedicated kid and had everything he needed to be a success. They went into the practice room, where the dancers were trying to grasp what was going on; they held the same opinion as the director and did not understand why he had run off. He even left his shoes behind, a pale young woman said. Zelda looked at the loafers in a corner and smiled to herself: they were the matches for the ones in Canizales' house, she placed them in a plastic bag and winked at Mendieta. They went out accompanied by the director. If he returns, let us know, we will thank you, above all, he will.

What do you make of it? In Culiacán or in Mazatlán they slept together and mixed up their shoes. There is a reason he ran. For sure he had time to go and return.

They drove around and had no luck. At Hotel La Siesta they found his personal effects. Nothing there. They picked up a photograph of the two embracing, all smiles, and a couple of notes scribbled on fine paper: "See you at 9 at L's house, bring the present. B" and "Please don't insist, I'll come to you when I'm ready. B" This last one looked like it had been crumpled and then ironed. Faint aromas. Mendieta pocketed them. A soft breeze entered through the big window facing the sea.

Zelda was anxious to hear some comment from her boss and since she could not see when it might be coming she asked. Well, it's true there are two key strikes against him, but the truth is fickle, it always hides behind a smokescreen, so we'd better wait for some proof, appearances mean something, but they're not decisive. Zelda did not agree, but she chose to remain silent. Everyone had told her Lefty was strange, but was rarely wrong. What about the silver bullet? I'd like to know about that, too.

"The bitter yellow sea of Mazatlán," as the poet called it, was filled with treasure hunters.

Captain Noriega, I'm calling to see if they do a good manta ray here in Mazatlán. Lefty, what are you doing here, plug-ugly? With this weather, who can resist the seashore? and we want a good meal. Who's with you? Shakira O'Neill. Black or white? Did you turn into a racist? No, just to get an image of her, though since she's with you she must be white. She's brown. O.K., do you remember where the Bahía is? Maybe. I'll see you there in fifteen minutes, I want Shakira's autograph, that is, if you don't hold exclusive rights. Noriega was the sharpest policeman on the Mazatlán force. They had taken that course on criminal investigation together in Tijuana, from which they came out worse than they went in according to Mendieta, but then he was hard to please. In reality they had spent the four days plus another two drinking and carousing with L.H., who they considered the most authentic bandit that ever existed.

Noriega was tall, dark, rather hefty, and he drank all the beer he could lay his hands on. It stimulates my intellect, he liked to say in his quick patter. What it stimulates is your belly, look at you. Do I look that bad? he asked Zelda, who blushed. Sitting down you can't tell. You see, don't try to contradict the official opinion of a woman as pretty as our colleague. Malú filled their table with dishes: shrimp in their shells, octopus, sea scallops, manta ray, and the incredible ceviche the place was famous for. They drank Pacífico and told him about the case and the dancer taking off, they gave him the photograph of Aldana with Bruno in case he turned up. If the lady will stay behind I'll help her search. That's not the plan, captain, that is, unless my boss has changed his mind. Do you want to stay? Of course she does, look at the way she's smiling just thinking about it. Indeed, Zelda was smiling: Boss, don't forget about Rodo, it means a lot to me. Her boyfriend's birthday, the detective said.

When? Saturday. Well, why doesn't he come on Saturday, that way you'll have time to miss each other while I show you how to fish for marlin, swordfish, and shark; you are a very special woman, to put up with this dolt is no small thing, a woman like you should learn about everything, oh, and for sure we'll find the dancer. Zelda kicked Mendieta under the table. Another time, for now I've got her busy over there, you know how short-staffed we are, why don't you come with us? My port would weep and so would I.

After the meal they said goodbye.

They reached the city at rush hour. Boss, I'm going to take a taxi to the Forum, I'll get something for Rodo and meet you at the office. Are you sure? There's a sale on that I don't want to miss. Call first, maybe you won't need to come.

On his desk he found a note from Ortega about the finger-prints on the supermarket bag and the cans: "They're Jack's". He also reported that the sodium rhodizonate test showed the Beretta had been fired by Paola Rodríguez. He was feeling so good after the trip that he decided not to telephone Dr Parra. Not totally confident, but hanging firm.

Before going home he stopped by the Guayabo. The band was playing a medley by the quartet from Liverpool. He drank three beers, two tequilas and left when the memory of his impossible love began to moisten his heart, only unsolvable problems are worth the effort, then he went over the events of the day: fucking dancer, and to think that he already had us won over.

Eighteen

Luigi, Mariana's dog, a black cocker spaniel with white markings, watched them from the carpet. Remember how we scared Paola? That was you, Sam, you know it suited me fine to have her running around with Canizales. I caught them naked and I tore a dozen strips off them, he couldn't find anything to say and there I was all lit up cursing them, threatening them, listing all the ways they were going to die; I grabbed her by the hair and dragged her. That you had not told me, remember you didn't want me following you, I stayed in the car. It was only a few metres along the hallway, I never imagined hair was that strong; Bruno begged me to let them get dressed, saying we should talk like civilised people; he was wrong, when love is at stake civilisation returns to the stone age and we go at each other with clubs: Civilised, your mother, I said and I gave him a slap in the face that wounded me to my soul, she was sort of distant, watching us argue, or rather she watched me howling and him trying to calm me down with that soft voice of his, using all that bullshit about tolerance they teach at the Universal Small Brotherhood, and me I was not about to let him off: You are such a jerk, you dare to ask me to be calm when you've been fucking this slut, and you, you better start praying, you fucking backstreet whore, because you're about to learn what real fire feels like, and she seemed to be in another dimension, looking at me, what was she on? that indifference was not normal, she looked like a statue, the skunk. I heard you scream and I got out of the car, I was desperate, it was the moment

I most wanted to be with you. Samantha did not speak, she had a bizarre feeling: she wanted to cry, to talk about Bruno, whom she was beginning to miss. That morning her son César had asked about him twice and she realised that she longed to see him, especially when César told her he had promised to take him rowing in Ernesto Millán Park. The first day of spring, that's not far off, right? She finished her gin. Fucking life, it's never what you expect. Mariana hugged her when she saw her eyes welling up. Uh-uh, she murmured, here in my house you're the butch and you are not going to break down, much less give in, because of that asshole. They were in the living room of Mariana's apartment on a white sofa facing a window, a breeze drifted in. The two of us did it, me more than you. Mariana Kelly was white with short black hair, she had a rough beauty about her, a pair of killer blue eyes, she was about twenty centimetres shorter than Samantha. They kissed softly. I don't understand myself either, Samantha murmured. Sam, you'll have to tell César, that would be best. Luigi wagged his tail.

The doorbell rang. They were expecting Ernesto Ponce, whom Mariana hated most cordially. Please Sam, five minutes, she insisted nervously. Samantha liked to make her suffer, liked rubbing salt in her jealous wounds whenever she could, so now she recovered quickly and thought that if the Gringo was looking handsome she would ask him to take her out for supper.

But the Gringo was dirty and worried, his jewellery made him look grotesque. Good evening, Señorita Samantha; Señorita Mariana, how are you? They were fine, thanks. So, what happened, why such a rush to see me, couldn't it wait until tomorrow? asked Samantha, while lighting a cigarette. Ponce sat across from them in a black leather chair, modernist style. You tell me, señorita, there are two things: first, your father doesn't want to pay for Tany's job and I'm afraid he'll find out everything about this mess; a few days ago I went to tell him and he wouldn't let me get the words out, yesterday afternoon he said no again, and then he said we had stirred up so much trouble he got a call from the district attorney's office. Those assholes, fucking leeches, sometimes I think that idiot Mendieta is right, we support the worst of the worst, what's the other thing? I have the distinct impression that Tany Contreras wasn't the one; he's always been a real talker, loves to boast about what he's done, how they beg him on their knees, and this time he said nothing. Maybe you took him down too soon. Ernesto Ponce looked at his hands: he saw his Magnum firing and Contreras falling from a bullet to the heart. Then his men castrated him and cut out his tongue. Late the night before Ponce had learned the hired gun had slept with the lover of one of his men and revenge was due. As you will understand, señorita, the matter has become complicated. You think so? well, I need that money. I also need my share, but I can't continue fooling your father, that would be fatal. Have they identified the body? Yes, but that's no problem, the boys picked it up and buried him in the countryside, do you want me to send a gift to Moisés Pineda for whatever he might be able to do? actually he had already done that. Let it lie, don't feed the pigs flowers; so, if it wasn't us, who was it? who killed Bruno Canizales? Mariana watched her intently. Unless somebody was also dying to get him, he committed suicide. Forget suicide, he was killed with a silver bullet and he didn't have any powder on his hands nor was there a gun in the house. Mariana relaxed, noted that ten minutes had passed, and winked at Samantha. Gringo, will you take me to dinner? Ponce choked: It would be a pleasure, señorita. Mariana was livid, but Samantha did not give a hoot, she grabbed her bag and stood up.

Luigi turned towards the Gringo and growled.

Nineteen

Mendieta's house in the Col Pop was owned by his brother Enrique. Three rooms on a single storey, kitchen, garage, living room, and a small garden at the back. Trudis woke him at seven: Alright, Lefty, get yourself up, would you like eggs with shredded beef? the water is hot for your Nescafé and I brought flour tortillas that are so tempting. I fell asleep at four, after three movies, a programme about the four hundredth anniversary of Don Quixote, and a special on John Lennon where Yoko Ono shows her tit. No matter, men should rise early, they've got to get themselves ready for work, I already cleaned your pistol and laid out your clothes. My pistol? It isn't the first time I've done it, don't forget my father was in the military and he showed me how. So, what time did you get here? I don't have a watch, what I earn is scarcely enough to feed myself and with everything costing the world what makes you think I would buy myself a watch; get up because soon I have to go to a meeting at the high school, it seems Marco Antonio is up to his old tricks. The guy from Los Bukis' kid? Well, whose else would he be, he looks just like him, his beard is starting to come in, the damn squirt, and you should hear his voice when he sings, lovely. What about your daughter? Which, Chespirito's or Vicente Fernández's? remember I have two. Chespirito's. She went to Mexico City to find her father, she's already written two plays, maybe he'll give her a hand, you wouldn't believe how funny they are, as soon as you start reading you're in tears you're laughing so hard, imagine if she gets to put them on. What I don't believe is the bit about Santana. I swear to God, it happened in Tijuana, he was so drunk he couldn't get it up, and Joan Manuel Serrat didn't feel like it, that man is a such a gentleman, how I would have liked to have his child, that time I didn't insist because I had my period, if not we'd have another composer in the family.

More tortillas? This is enough. I'm going to pour you more coffee, that work of yours takes a lot of energy, so don't you go leaving anything on your plate, and Lefty, go shave, you aren't the kind of person to go about like a penniless bum, yesterday I let you go because there was no time, but today you aren't leaving until you're presentable, how did it go in Mazatlán? It went, listen, don't think you can get me back into the bathroom. Why not? you leave here looking respectable or you don't leave, period, your blessed mother would not forgive me if you went out with that face. You can't win, he stood up and went off to shave.

As soon as he turned on the cell phone: cavalry charge. Mendieta. Fucking killjoy, why did you take the chick with you? she would have had such a good time, to begin with she would have been nice and warm in bed, all her needs attended to. She confessed to me she likes you, she said she'll stay with you when you lose twenty kilos, the way you are now she's afraid you'd have a heart attack, what news? Your dancer hasn't shown his face anywhere, but he hasn't left the port, last night we did a roundup on Crestón Hill, where the lighthouse is, we interrogated all the detainees and nothing, they hadn't even heard of him. O.K., send me the report by email. I'd rather Zelda Toledo came for it. Alright, but send it to me first.

*

At the office he had a message from Guillermo Ortega. He went over to his cubicle next to the lab, which was overflowing with the residue of hundreds of cases. What's up, faggot? listen, before I forget, my son needs to do a report on *Pedro Páramo*, that's a book you ought to have, could you lend it to him? You sure turned out cheap, buy him one, it won't even cost you a hundred pesos. But if you have one, why should I spend the money? So you'll have at least one book in your house. No way, suppose the kid turns into an intellectual, what a fucking curse that would be. The book is fairly dangerous, you're right, but I don't think anything is going to happen, that poor kid is so much like you I'd wager a testicle he'll barely read the cover. For all I've missed by not reading it, I don't think the little dummy is wrong, however I'd rather not run the risk, so you are going to lend it to him and shut your trap; O.K., there are two pieces of information I want to give you, even though I know you're worthless and you'll never find the culprit. The culprits find me. Well, while you're waiting for that to happen, I don't want things held up on our account, so here you go: both copies of *News from the Empire*, the one I gave you and the one I have here have too many fingerprints from Paola Rodríguez; the one I gave you was hers if I remember right, it also has his prints and some unknown; on the silver bullets, there is a factory in Tucson, here's the address and the telephone; now kiss my balls and don't forget Memo's book. I'm surprised he didn't download his report from Google. He did, but that twit of a teacher caught him. Didn't I tell you, a knucklehead just like his dad. O.K., jerk-off, don't step over the line, don't start in on my family. Come on, do you really still believe he's yours?

He left the room wanting a smoke.

At his desk he lit up.

He tried to make sense of his notes on the Palm: "cas Brun Caniz Paol sem m bod". What is this? "Ripal aer 47. perfume, so&n Agric min,gv susp, Pao Rodrig, F aldan,p3 Yoonohoo Vald, M Kell, Saman Val, Laura, 17-46Z%&f!?tQ". This sucker must have caught a virus. He turned it off and tossed it into the right-hand drawer. I can't deal with technology. If Laura Frías is right, the murderer could be any of the ones she named, including Paola Rodríguez, who more than made good on her threat; let's see, I've got Paola, Samantha, Mariana, Frank Aldana, Yoonohoo Valdés. The people from the U.S.B. could also have done it: Ripalda, Figueroa, Dania, and Laura herself. The way things are today, you've got to suspect even the guy everyone adores, and of what? Of godliness, to say the least, if not hypocrisy. They killed John Lennon, so why wouldn't they kill this loser, no-one can be on good terms with everyone, if he was, he wouldn't have been rubbed out. Somebody new? Laura claimed to know nothing about that, but since the guy was friendly we can't rule it out. A killer hired by the father? Motive: to win the big chair. It's possible, why? what feelings does a man like Bruno awaken in the people around him? A sugar cube on some days, an insufferable jerk on others, according to Beatriz, affectionate with children, good lover, good friend; I should talk to his mother, since he called her to tell her he was happy.

A human being is so many things. Crime of passion, vengeance? The suspects so far fit the bill, except it was a bullet to the head and no sign of struggle; such respect for the body and the immediate surroundings indicates something else, no profanation, and what about the silver bullets? and the fragrance? was there ever a murderer around here who used silver bullets? He did not know. I have to call Tucson. Every killer is sending a message, what's this one's? what is he trying to prove? who is he defying? he lit another cigarette, society? the police? Did he own something? land, houses, works of art? did he have a will?

Zelda came in with a Diet Coke: Want some? It rusts my insides. He called Tucson.

After two female voices, he was put through to Mr Gary Cooper, general manager of Tucson Weapons, Ltd. This is Detective Edgar Mendieta of the Federal Preventive Police in Mexico, I'm going to ask you a few questions. It's been years since I've been to Mexico, last time I was there I drove down, the highways were awful, full of dead dogs, they seemed like backstreets. The detective ignored the comment and went right to the point: How many Mexican customers do you have? I will not give out the names of my clients, nor the number, who do you think you are? All I want to know if anyone buys from you. More than you would imagine, I won't say any more than that, I won't waste my time talking to the most corrupt police force in the world. How many in Sinaloa? Maybe twenty, and as I said I will not give you a single name. All of them buy silver bullets? You are an idiot, the stupidest policeman I have ever spoken to in my life. You can repeat that to the boys from Interpol who are dying to pay you a visit. Let them come, I do everything by the book and you have no right to harass me. Mendieta changed tactics: Let me apologise, Mr Cooper, I thank you for your cooperation, it turns out that we have a nutcase here killing Americans with silver bullets and the F.B.I. asked for our cooperation, what you have told me is sufficient and since I'm sure you like hunting, I promise to take you to the Siete Gotas Mountains where there are plenty of deer, ocelots, and lynx. I've heard about that place. Well, free up your calendar for November when the season opens, you'll be the guest of the Federal Preventive Police. I understand, give me an email address; oh, and tell your friends from Interpol that I cooperated. No need to worry, the Mexican police have everything under control.

An hour later he printed out a list of eighteen names.

He looked the first one up in the telephone directory, Carlos Alvarado. Culiacán Farms, a woman answered. Señor Alvarado, please. The elder or the younger. The elder. He heard a friendly voice: How can I help you. My name is Bond, James Bond, he thought, but he said: Edgar Mendieta, from the State Ministerial Police, you buy silver bullets in Tucson, what do you use them for? Ah, you had me scared, when the police call it could be anything, please don't take offence; yes certainly, about five years ago I went with my compadre Federico Villegas, may he rest in peace, to Tucson, he liked to give those bullets as gifts and I bought a box, I still have it, unopened, if you'd like to come by and see it, I've got it in a display case as a curiosity. How long ago did your compadre pass away? It's going to be three years. Could you give me the telephone of one of his relatives? Sure, my comadre Ernestina, 513-98-31, she lives in Chapule on Dr Romero Street, they own Villegas Farm Tools, a long-standing business in the valley. Do you know of anyone else who likes to shoot silver bullets? We all like shooting, but these are expensive, five years ago I paid thirty dollars a bullet, can you imagine, just for a gift. I thank you for your cooperation, Don Carlos. Excuse me, Lieutenant Mendieta, before we say good-bye, is there any news on the death of Engineer Canizales' son?

Don't tell anyone, but we are about to zap the murderer. We're anxious to stay on top of developments in the case, lieutenant, since we all want the Engineer in the Palace, right? It's the perfect place for him. That's what we farmers think. Thank you again, Don Carlos. Whatever I can do to help, captain, we are here to serve you.

Zelda and Angelita located the rest. Eleven deceased, and except for Don Carlos and his comadre Ernestina de Villegas, who was away on a trip, they all had moved to the United States and it would cost a fortune to find them. They checked the names and none of them had a criminal record, none was young, and all were from traditionally powerful families. If we are going to get anywhere it won't be with that obsolete list, could there be another? where do young people buy their munitions? He saw it was impossible and decided to abandon that angle for the moment. They would try another route. He reminded himself that no expert follows the evidence, since in this business the truth always resides precisely where it should not.

With that thought in mind he returned to Canizales' house.

What was he seeking? He wished he knew.

Twenty

Figueroa took the floor: I have called you here early, because I believe we have to do something to make sure that whoever killed our colleague Bruno Canizales gets what he deserves, the police are so incompetent if we let things lie they are likely to drop the case. Brown-skinned, thin, dressed in white. We must not allow that to occur, we should write to the newspapers, get on the radio and talk up the issue, let's make sure everyone knows about it; I suggest we name two committees, one to speak to the Human Rights Commission and the other to sit down with the policeman in charge or with the girl, Agent Toledo, his assistant; if they play deaf we shall go to their superiors, whoever they are, or to the district attorney. In a white room at the U.S.B. centre about ten people listened without interest; only Laura Frías and Dania Estrada were paying attention, the latter took the floor: We agree, our organisation must not remain passive in the face of this tragedy, though we can't bring back our friend, we must not allow the crime to go unpunished, Laura and I will speak with the policeman and with Agent Toledo, the one who took our statements at Bruno's house; so, who would like to volunteer to write a letter to the editor? No-one. A fly landed on a shoe. How about a volunteer to go to Human Rights? No-one either. I will write the letter, Figueroa conceded, I'll take it to Human Rights in memory of our colleague and to maintain the good name of the U.S.B., and now let's move on to other business, the first item is should Dr Ripalda continue coming? Since no-one offered an opinion, Figueroa himself said yes, because meditation is very important for spiritual growth and in the new world everyone will have to do it; for the time being Ripalda could stay at his house. He then spoke at length about global warming and holes in the ozone layer and no-one paid him the least attention.

Leaving the meeting, Laura called Mendieta's number, but his cell phone was off.

Twenty-One

Three in the afternoon. The sun was bright. In the México bookstore on Obregón Avenue he bought a copy of *Pedro Páramo*. Before reaching Canizales' house he stopped at Cotorra de la R for a ceviche with two beers and a conch dish, which did not sit well. As Rudy says, he reflected, for a meal to be really good it has to do a bit of harm.

He parked across from the entrance. The yellow tape was on the ground and there were no guards. Without getting out, he contemplated the door, the open garage, the car, the flowers, the white fence. Here, they killed a man a few days ago, he thought, someone who knew him went in that door and shot him, someone he trusted, did he come in with him? was he waiting inside or out? did he turn up later? why? Though it is tempting to think Aldana is guilty because he's a scaredy-cat, something tells me he was not the one; murderers lack something he has in spades: the ability to grieve. Besides, it does not look like a crime of passion; of course killers know how we categorise them, did he straighten things up? Right, fucking Palm, I'll have to use a notebook. Perfume. The criminal came in with him and killed him before he even got into his pyjamas; no, he was waiting for him; no, he killed him on his feet and held him up, then he laid him down. Too bad Montaño could not analyse his gastric juices or other body fluids, but it would have turned out the same, I suspect; that sort of evidence won't help pinpoint the murderer in this case. The gunshot was so well placed he must have taken it without a struggle; was there powder on his face? I mean, if they shot him point-blank it would have left something; and suppose it was the narcos? They would have made a huge mess, especially if Yoonohoo Valdés sent them, since he runs everything, he does not know the meaning of the word "moderation". We are not going to find out about the powder either. Paola, did you kill him and then kill yourself the way you swore you would? Tell me. But you called after 4.30, what for? Of course, because it wasn't you. Who sells silver bullets in this city? Don Carlos has them all. Mariana Kelly was born in Guadalajara, in May she'll turn thirty-four. Could she be the one who got hold of the munitions? Did someone hire a hit man? Which one or ones not in the picture ordered the kill? The father who wants to be president, the brother who imitated him, the lawyer who is a bastard, the U.S.B. people, Laura, a housebreaker, his assistant Alfaro, a kid he picked up on Sinaloa Boulevard, how about me, the gangsta-wraps, Zelda, Pineda. We're all guilty until proven innocent. I ought to interrogate Yoonohoo Valdés.

He got out of the car and went to look at the sedan parked in the garage. Inside, above some wilted roses, a red light was winking insistently. The windshield was dirty, caked with dead insects, typical highway filth, the front grille the same; him so neat and the car is disgusting. He wrote in his little notebook: "dirty car". One day I'll learn how to use the Palm. He opened the blue door to the house, where the lab found Jack the Ripper's prints, in other words all the possible prints in the world and good luck finding the culprit's. In the living room he admired the Kijano painting, grey tones around a redheaded nymph. Every brushstroke was an homage to life, to sensuality, to the pleasures of being human. Paola Rodríguez? It could be. Even though the figure was tiny, in the redhead's eyes the artist managed to capture the emptiness evident in the photographs in her bedroom.

Would you go to bed with a depressive? No way, I like women who talk and talk tough.

The guest bedroom was impeccable, untouched. So was the bathroom. Nothing out of place. The study same story. The new computer still boxed up in the same place. He opened the drawers one by one. Not many papers. He paused at the December telephone bill. Local calls, long distance to Mexico City and to Palm Springs on the twenty-fourth. He put it in his pocket.

The bedroom where they found the body still looked the same, they had not even taken the sheets off the chair or cleaned up. He went over it all, first in his mind and then in the reality in front of his eyes. He had a feeling the two did not quite match, but he could not see how.

He called Guillermo Ortega's cell phone. No answer. Then he called Ortega's house. His wife said he was in the middle of a nap. Sarita, get him up if you would, I have an urgent request. Lefty, what's got into all of you, you're going to kill the man, he barely rests, poor thing, it seems people get themselves killed more than ever and my poor husband has to be on every case, don't you think he's sick and tired of seeing gangsta-wraps every day? Please, Sarita, it'll be quick, he can answer my question and then go back to sleep, I promise. You, you, just because you don't have anyone who takes care of you. Come on, don't be difficult, he must have already had his nap. Lefty, you are so inconsiderate. This had better be something important, it was Ortega's voice. Are you awake? This bird-brain woke me up with her yelling. O.K., the question: Did you look at Canizales' car? I think so, a Vectra '04 or '05, clean as a whistle inside, covered in spiderwebs outside, I'll send you the results in a little while. What about the other rooms? Yes, but we didn't find anything, you know they practically threw us out. Listen, do me a big favour, there is a fragrance that is bothering me, I detected it in Canizales' bedroom and I can't forget it, it's still there, a strange aroma, strong, spicy, maybe you can help us. Why do you get so much pleasure out of making me work double? To keep your belly from growing. It's something else that's growing. Thanks, old buddy, sweet dreams.

As he entered his office, cavalry charge: What are you up to, lazy-bones? Working like an idiot, this year I'm going to win a gold star for sure. Didn't you turn out ambitious, and especially with that little boss they've given you, eh? Don't criticise my boss, asshole, you don't know him, he's the best conciliator in the world. And he's got a face like my balls. That is something only you and he would know. Listen, here's the news, your dancer vanished and I've got to work on a case of two fishermen at sea found full of lead from A.K.s, you can imagine where this one is headed; this morning I went to the dance school and talked to Aldana's classmates, listen, what great chicks they've got there, for the love of God, I could care less about a heart attack, I came out of there like a deer in the headlights, that director is a honey. You ought to sign up for a class. Your mother should take it, may she rest in peace, they laughed; in any case they thought he seemed normal the whole time, on Friday he was worn out like the rest of them, one thought she had seen him around midnight coming out of the Shrimp Bucket with a guy a little taller than him, but she's not sure; by the clock he could easily have gone to Culiacán to commit the murder and got back; he ate a lot in the Café Altazor, the owner's a journalist who is always in a bad mood, I asked him and he said he saw him run out of the school, climb into an open-air taxi, a "pneumonia", and disappear towards the docks; that's all. I thank you for it. I hope you understand that I'm accumulating brownie points so you'll bring me your partner Toledo, I like her behind, and those pointy little tits so she can nurse me the way I should have been. Sure. What was that woman doing in Traffic? She helped people cross the street. Whose idea was it to bring her over to the police? Mine, she has a spatial intelligence most of us would die for. Except you, who even went to university. And you who walked by it. Well, that's another reason why we'd understand each other, we'll get married and have many children with spatial intelligence and you will be their lucky godfather, listen, what happened to the blonde? What blonde? Kiss my balls, jerk-off, keep playing the fool and you'll see where it gets you. Don't exaggerate. See you later. Don't forget your sunscreen.

Angelita from the doorway: Boss, a Señor Abelardo Rodríguez is here to see you, he says he is Paola's father, can I get you anything? If you go to the Oxxo bring me a coffee, he handed her a bill, where is Zelda? She went for her Diet Coke, could you spring for one for me? Even two if you want.

Señor Rodríguez came in wearing his khaki work clothes and steel-toed boots, smelling of alcohol. A promise is a debt, Lieutenant Mendieta, here is the permit, I can leave it with you or make a copy. Sit down for a moment, Señor Rodríguez, would you like a cold drink? Do you have coffee? I don't recommend it, our budget barely allows for coloured water. That's no problem, he sat in a small chair to one side of a table on which a broken computer was collecting dust. You know I always carry my supply with me, the insinuation went unacknowledged. I see you are working. Despite my grief life goes on, how is the case of Attorney Canizales coming? It's got feet of lead, the shooter turned out to be a slippery one, but he's going to fall for sure. I heard on "Eyes on the Night" that you're onto him. Those journalists live in a fantasy world, don't believe them. Well, I hope the case gets solved and it won't affect the engineer, who as you must know is looking to be his party's new candidate for the big chair. He would be the ideal candidate. They just need to let him. Señor Rodríguez, I still have a couple of questions about the death of your daughter, I didn't want to bother you, but since you are here: Do you think there is a connection between the two deaths, hers and the attorney's? I've thought so much about it, you know what Beatriz says about her threatening to do it if he left her and all that, but I just can't believe it. The guy was killed with a silver bullet. Well, there you go, where would my daughter get one of those? Where did Paola learn to shoot? I taught her when she was young, we were building a house in the mountains and she spent several days there practising; then I realised she was depressive and I regretted it, unfortunately there was no way back. The night before her death, did you speak with her? No, in fact she didn't have supper with us, there were problems between her and her mother and she often preferred to eat alone. Did you go out that night or did you go to bed early? I went out to the office about nine, I had to close a deal

112

in Tijuana around that time, you know over there it's an hour earlier, and my computer at home doesn't have a webcam; I came back at midnight more or less. Was someone with you in your office? The watchman, he answered everything with aplomb. Señor Rodríguez, thank you very much, leave the permit with me, please, I'll bring it to your house later on. Although we are suffering with our sorrows, it will be a pleasure to offer you a drink in a proper glass, those plastic ones were practically an insult. Delighted to repeat the experience, is your wife O.K.? She'll get over it, the one I see as sadder is my daughter, she's asking permission to study theatre in Mexico City. It is hard to lose a member of the family. They were really tight, those girls, so I'll probably let her go, if I wasn't able to pay for Paola to go to Spain, for Beatriz I'll make the effort. That seems a wise decision. Ah, the play she's in is called "My Dearest Girl", I saw it yesterday. Do you recommend it? Not really, too much groping and that's my daughter up there. They said goodbye.

The permit had been issued by the National Defence Secretariat and was valid.

He felt no desire to remain at the office and it was too early to go for a drink. He tried to clear his mind by going through the notebook, but it was worse than the Palm. What is happening to me, have I turned into a moron? So he slipped out and twenty-two minutes later he was at the movies watching "Capote". He tried to buy popcorn, but a shiver ran down his spine.

Twenty-Two

Six o'clock in the morning. Minerva entered her husband's tiny office carrying a steaming mug of coffee. Valdés was going over the accounts in a hundred-page school notebook, the desk was covered with bundles of dollars in different denominations. Good morning, how is the man of the house? Even the aroma is killing me, the old man picked up the mug and savoured his first sip. Would you like to drink it here? because you have a visitor. Who? Hildegardo Canizales, he says he has an appointment. That's right, call Ulysses, tell him to make the payments as usual and deposit the rest in any of the three banks I indicate and then make the transfer. Cayman Islands or Switzerland? United States, it's safer there, he knows, if he has any questions it's all in here, he tapped the notebook sitting on top of the money. Send the engineer to the bungalow in the garden. Are we going to give him our support? We'll see what he has to offer. Don't raise his hopes too high, you know what they say about that bungalow: whoever you meet in there gets everything he wants. Come on, I met with the others in there. I wouldn't want you to get shanghaied. By the way, I think we won't be moving to the country. Why? The waters are all whipped up, I learned last night that the federal government is about to get nasty. So? So I can't disappear until I negotiate the new rules. What are you going to do? I'll propose legalisation, he smiled. Do you think they'll listen? Of course not, he smiled again. I understand.

*

Engineer Hildegardo Canizales accepted the drug lord's condolences with a contrite gesture: Thank you, Don Marcelo, he was my pride, a fine boy with a promising future; it is difficult to accept the ways of the Lord, but what can we do? Carry on, engineer, there is no alternative, life continues and so do we, tell me what's on your mind. They sat down, Valdés served his guest coffee from a Thermos and drank from his own mug, the bodyguards were on alert. Members of the three wings of my party are interested in my running for the big chair, after the funeral of my son they came to my home with the proposal, at first I told them no and they smiled, I had to promise to think about it, they insisted that there was nothing to think about, he paused, Valdés watched him, his face a blank, I let them know that I could not make such an important decision without consulting you and that is the motive of my visit. Valdés gave an approving nod, sipped his coffee: It would be extraordinary if we could have you in the chair, the guy from your party who is running now I don't like one bit. Well, it is your decision, from now on the matter is in your hands. The drug lord nodded, understood that Canizales would make a good candidate, at least better than the others who had turned up looking for support, and far superior to the one who was at that moment out campaigning; maybe it would be worth risking the two billion it would cost to put a hopeful in the chair. Maybe. Engineer, I welcome your aspirations and I am prepared to invest whatever it takes, I am only going to impose one condition. You are in charge, Don Marcelo, I said as much and I repeat it. I want the bankers and business in too, they never risk a thing, but when the pie comes out of the oven they always show up expecting their slice, and as you well know they never say they've had enough.

You can count on it, Don Marcelo. I will send you a list so you'll know exactly who it is I want in. They drank again. There is one point that bothers me, engineer, now his face was hard, if we are going to go for the big chair, I don't think it is in your interest to have the matter of your son in the media every day. That can be fixed, Señor Valdés, don't worry, District Attorney Bracamontes is dreaming of a promotion and he would do anything to get it. Well, that would not be at all bad.

When they left the bungalow, Canizales looked radiant. That is what the Gringo saw from the doorway of the small office where he was helping Ulysses carry the suitcases stuffed with bills.

Valdés looked happy too.

Twenty-Three

When he exited the Citicinema he turned on the cell phone and immediately the familiar cavalry charge rang out. Boss, where are you hiding? I went to Mass. You aren't out drinking this early in the day, are you? I'm practically a teetotaller, I'm an anachronism. Well, don't overdo it; listen, two things: don't forget that on Saturday I'm going out with Rodo to celebrate his b-day, we'll probably leave the city, do you think I could take Friday afternoon off? We'll see, what's the other thing? Mariana Kelly called, she says she's ready to see you, she'll expect you tonight at her house at nine, do you want me to go along? No, you call Laura Frías and pay her a visit at home, maybe she didn't tell me everything she knows about Canizales, sniff around a bit there. What are we looking for? I don't know, they call them clues, but I really don't know what, use your head; did Mariana leave her number? Write it down. Call her, tell her I'll be there, did Ortega send anything? Oh, yes, on the front and back yards, and on the car and the garage; the one on the car is interesting, they found tollbooth receipts from the Culiacán–Mazatlán highway from the night he was killed, they had them in a bag they hadn't looked at, what do you think. Interesting, I'm tempted to say Aldana didn't come to him, it was Canizales who took to the road. But he's still guilty, isn't he? Of course, we will never forgive him for what he did to us. I'm going to leave the report on your desk. And don't worry about all this, take it easy so you'll have plenty of energy for Saturday, oh, and get me a date with the mother, I'd like to hear what's behind her accusation. By the way, I went back to Social Security, Mónica Alfaro wasn't in but one of the secretaries told me that on the fatal day, before Bruno left, a young man came in, furious, and let him have it for dumping him, he threatened to kill himself. Another who thinks he couldn't live without him, what is wrong with these people? why do they think they're indispensable? find out where he lives and tomorrow we'll pay him a visit, for now go see Laura. And don't you start carousing. The way the world is going soon we'll all be Chinese, so we'd better run wild while we still can; oh, call Rodríguez's office, ask the watchman how late the boss was there Thursday night. O.K., give me a call if you need me; here's a tip, six months ago Mariana Kelly took a target shooting course in Phoenix.

After a few minutes, the cell phone rang again, the detective was still in the movie-theatre parking lot mulling over "Capote", the topic of homosexual relations invariably evoked unwanted memories, Bardominos dressed in white, his shirt buttoned right to the top button. Mendieta. Can I see you? Of course, is there something new? I want to pressure you to find whoever killed Bruno. What do you have in mind? Maybe a massage called "It'll Hurt"? I'll pass. The bottom line is we don't want our friend's murder to go unpunished. Tell the people who asked you to lean on me that we are doing the impossible and that we're making good progress. And suppose I tell you it was my idea? You'd be lying and putting your good name at risk, what I do agree is that we ought to meet up, I'd like you to tell me more about Canizales' relationship with Samantha Valdés, how about we have breakfast tomorrow at nine. Where? At the Miró, you can have another salad. And you another disgusting sandwich, could we make it at eleven?

They were smiling when they said goodbye. The detective thought it was time to learn something about the parents, beyond the official story.

The lighting where Mariana Kelly lived was soft. He parked in the street and took the elevator to the third floor. Forest fragrance. Goga Fox opened the door and he almost peed his pants. He had fallen into a trap, should he draw his gun? scream as loud as he could? call for reinforcements? Nope, any attempt would be useless.

Thirteen months before.

At a party in Altata, invited by Omar Briseño who had just been promoted, he saw her for the first time. Gorgeous, like the first night with the love of your life. Tall, delicate and sensual features, platinum blonde hair cut very short. She was chatting with the other wives while the men talked business, politics, soccer. She must be married to one of these yokels, he thought, and he felt nervous just looking at her. She listened attentively to her companions, encouraged them with a playful smile or a cautious nod. On the fourth whisky Mendieta went out to the beachfront where two large boats were moored, and over to the beach lit subtly by a spotlight spattered with sand and more by the full moon. The night sea is a remote past, he thought, inscrutable but in motion, filled with Portuguese sailors led by Ferdinand Magellan going around the day in eighty worlds. The sea is a good place to be a man and not die in the attempt.

Sorry, I must have made a mistake, he muttered, his heart leaping into his dry mouth. Edgar Mendieta, aren't you going to say hello? He wanted to kiss her, strip off her clothes, make love to her right then and there the way the inventor of sliding doors must have imagined; to watch once again her lean body making its way towards the bathroom with that unbelievable killer stride; she had the strange habit of washing herself immediately after sex and thus that palm-leaf sashay. What a surprise, he kissed her on the right cheek. In Europe they kiss both and people get upset when you kiss only one, she brought her face near, he obeyed. The same perfume. The red skirt, the white blouse with the persimmon print. Memories bouncing on a ping-pong table. The aroma, the smile, her eyes all made his head spin; that particular fragrance, made from rose essence and what was the other ingredient? He felt it in his stomach.

Either you're sad or you're a poet. Under the moon on the beach he did not know whether to look at her resplendent hair or her smile. Why not a sculptor? You look calmer than the others, shall we go for a stroll? Back in those days, thanks to Dr Parra, he had his anxieties completely under control. My name is Edgar Mendieta and I am about to turn into a werewolf. Georgina Fox, they call me Goga, what should I do so you won't attack me? Speak nicely. I see, you are one of those guys who thinks having a woman at his side makes the world turn. Mendieta was not one of those. On the contrary, I think that if women ruled the world everything would be chaos. Even more than it is already, I don't think so. Have you ever drunk Goga-Cola? No, does such a thing exist? It's a thick clear drink, comes in sweet or sour. Where do they sell it, I've got to try it. I'll let you know, he wanted to tell her that she smelled fabulous, but he did not dare, what happens when you compliment a woman's perfume? He did not know.

He was about to repeat that he had made a mistake, but behind Goga he saw Samantha Valdés and Mariana Kelly, looking mischievous: Hello, commander, how goes the heroic life? are you an anonymous hero or an eponymous one? Good evening, Mariana's smile was cold and there were deep circles under her eyes. No matter how much of a bastard you are you can't complain about this reception, right detective? Samantha fixed him with a glare, they were on their way out; behind Goga, Luigi wagged his tail. Dear, we have errands to do, a couple of guys to kill with silver bullets, and certainly you two would like to continue catching up, so if you know how to count, don't count on us, oh, and the dog is well-trained, as soon as he sees two people kiss, he disappears. Then they left them there, at the door, did he feel like bawling them out? it did not even cross his mind, was he going to stop them before they got on the elevator? not that either, should he go away and have a few drinks to clear his mind? dear God, what labyrinths you spin for your children. Every human chews his pencils. He stood there watching them move off and then he turned towards Goga, who was making way for him with a flourish.

A week after that first encounter, his mouth dry and his heart pounding, he was waiting in the parking lot of Ley Tres Ríos supermarket at 9.20 as they had agreed. He saw her get out of an Audi A6, give her shopping list to a kid in a black beret, and walk towards the white Jetta: white print blouse, red skirt with flounces: a stupendous sign.

I had no idea you knew each other. Since we were girls, when we were all classmates at Monfe. Have they been lovers since then? You cut right to the chase, I guess you aren't losing your touch as a detective, she put ice in two glasses and served whisky, the answer is yes; Mariana was always sure, Samantha less so, that's why she got married and had, as she says, that awful experience with her husband; but they never stopped being together and they still are, to your health, because you look the same. To yours, he was going to say, because he found her even lovelier, but he had not yet recovered. Luigi, beside the easy chair, looked at them expectantly.

She did not want to go to a motel, but since he had no friends who could lend them a house they ended up in one. They opened the door and welcomed each other with kisses: kisses that made their eyelids, their skin, their pubic hair stand on end, that hid their commitments, their dreams, that stripped them of their clothes, their future, their intelligence. Firm, perfumed body, precise breasts, and her way of being revealed. Everything that orgasms, half-open lips, and closed eyes give away. She got up and headed towards the bathroom and for the first time he saw that magnificent behind on the way to being washed.

Goga gave him a velvet kiss, but he remained cold, untamed, disconcerted. He saw Parra's beard giving him advice and a dark room. Deep down he hoped to keep his distance, felt he had suffered too much, as if he had never read *Love in the Time of Cholera*. They sat down together across from the dog.

I can see you're still mad at me, she said looking him in the eyes. Mendieta looked at his hands and swirled his glass, he knew he was weak, lacking the right words to express his confusion. When did you get back? The detective sipped his drink, his heart galloping. Monday night, black suits you, I've told you that before, haven't I? He nodded. When your thoughts are racing you never know which one to utter, he wanted to tell her that he understood the message of her attire, but he remained tongue-tied. I understand, she said, and she tossed back her drink in one swallow.

For four months they had seen each other once a week. He was happy. For the first time in many years he had managed to clear out the cobwebs, she revelled in him. One day she went away. He went up and down her street, staked out her empty house, became a regular at the Miró, and even the kid with the black beret was witness to his distress. The worst: one night Bardominos came back stronger than ever and he went back to Parra. I hope you agree I'm in a desperate plight. He was so deeply hung up on her that he believed enduring it without looking for her was a heroic stance. It turned out her husband had become a producer in Hollywood and they were living in Los Angeles, it was a true feat to keep from buying an all-inclusive and zipping off to find her.

I live in Santa Monica, she served herself another drink, I'll be here for two weeks and now we have the night before us, the girls will sleep at Samantha's house, any proposal no matter how improper will be accepted, she made herself comfortable on the sofa revealing 87 per cent of her legs. My werewolf. Mendieta saw his world was crumbling. The ancients were right, the world is flat and it ends in a great waterfall, what was that song she used to sing? what I would have given for this to have happened six months ago, "I have witnesses: a dog, the dawn, the cold", it's too late, he thought, he was not a womaniser, he stood up, terrified: I'm leaving, it's been a pleasure seeing you, truly, he paused, I can't stay, I can't go against my convictions. Edgar, you have no reason to leave, we're mature adults, capable of being ourselves in any context, of seeing our relationship clearly, but he was not listening, did not want to, could not, he left his glass on a sideboard, opened the door, and went down the stairs without seeing that Luigi would not stop wagging his tail.

He went to the bar in the Hotel Lucerna, where he drank and cried like a man, alongside a bunch of inflamed soccer fans watching the Mexican side go down to the United States on penalties.

Well, yeah, no way, no nothing.

Twenty-Four

Twelve midnight. Copper, is that you? Who else? Christina Aguilera, for example, who is about to give birth to my child. Oh. Are you drunk, copper? How could you think that, what's on your mind? When I woke up today I suffered an attack of decency, it got worse all day, and right now I can't hold out any longer, I want to be of service to society. You don't say. Don't ask. Did you call the Humane Society? I tried to tell them, but they sent me to you, to Lefty Mendieta, the flashiest badge in town. Do you want to confess? The fact is you're tripping over your tongue, copper my man, is something wrong? Nothing, I'm listening. Let's see you do a D.U.I. step. Come on, spill it, why are you calling me so late? The night they killed the enemy I was near his house and maybe I heard a gunshot and saw who did it, do you hear me? Go on. I blew you away, don't try to fake it, why did you get drunk? A woman. Same as me, but I got over it and I advise you to do the same, would you like a snort or are you just a romantic copper loyal to your weed. Don't you know I could lock you away for fifteen years for hiding information and seven more for drug addiction? Don't you know my father would spring me in seven minutes on either charge? Who's he? A maiden fair with scraggly hair, you look into it, copper my man, you're deep into your cups for some reason, did your babe die too? Practically. That is hell itself, ain't it, copper, in my bitch of a life I never felt so shitty, that's why I want you to make the arrest so you'll get named copper of the month and they'll give you a cheque so you'll never lack for your

125

nose candy or your lager and you'll be able to bear your sorrows. That's up to you. I'm not going to tell you over the telephone, there might be a little bird on the line, I'll only say that the day they cooked the stew I saw the queen at home, it would have been 3.30 in the morning, I climbed aboard my little bike and off I went, you can imagine where I was headed, I staked out the house of the enemy, but he never showed, what I did see is going to cost you a pretty penny, how about half the cheque they're going to give you? That sounds fair. You tell me where to meet you, oh, and let's do it tomorrow because right now I'm reading, do you know what my babe left me as inheritance? a book. And you think that woman loved you? anyone who gets you reading hates you from the depths of her being. Shut your trap, copper, shut it. Did you see the murderer go in or come out? What's with you, copper my man, don't get pushy, tomorrow I'll spill the beans, but let's make it in the afternoon because in the morning I'm going to be busy being decent. You don't say. Don't ask, as you like to say. Why not now? Because it's time for something else, something sweeter and nicer. At six in the Miró. Make it seven at Las Ventanas, death to the bad guys.

Twenty-Five

Trudis interrupted him: Lefty, you're late, I'm going to read you your horoscope while you get yourself together, "Capricorn: Anything related to learning is in your favour, your planets are aligned to give you good fortune, and your financial situation will improve as long as you think of yourself as rich; in romance, although you ought to keep your heart open, you should remain cautious, an old flame will turn up and who knows if you have the strength to face him or her. If you are a gambler, bet on number eight and choose red, it will pay off." How about that? only as soon as you get the dough don't forget about your Trudis; listen, I've got your 7 Up with lemon all ready, I'm saying, because you look like the Indians dragged you off, shall I bring it in? Please, he could not read, could barely see the letters in *News from the Empire* for thinking about her.

He ate eggs à la mexicana before turning on his cell phone, which always marked the beginning of his workday. He called Zelda Toledo: Get an arrest order and bring Mariana Kelly in. Did she get away from you? Worse, I nearly got killed. Where do I get one? Write it, sign it, and carry it out, at eleven I'm seeing Laura Frías at the Miró, so do it an hour later, any news? Well, everyone here is laughing at you. No kidding, what did I do now? Someone sent you a bouquet of red roses and the whole Headquarters smells of it. It's yours, a gift, put it on your desk. You had that one well hidden, didn't you, boss? Don't speculate, Agent Toledo, did you visit Laura

127

Frías? Last night, that bit of gossip almost made me forget. She told him that Laura had served her guava juice and whole-wheat crackers, that she had not added much, except for two details that could be important. Did you know that Bruno's father wants to be president? Don Carlos Alvarado said something about it, that he could take the place of the party's current candidate. Well, he's deep into it and something like a month ago he asked Bruno to rein himself in, he didn't want to get attacked for having a homosexual son. Listen to that, and he tells me he hasn't spoken to him in four years. Something else, boss, lately Bruno took to dressing up as a woman, Laura kept the clothes at her house, she showed me, lovely things. What would he do? Apparently he would go to parties and maybe out on a date with somebody, she couldn't tell me more. I should talk to his mother, see if she'll see me today.

Ortega on the line: What's up, faggot, I already heard, you should do a better job of acting the part, pretty soon people will think everyone on the force is letting rain in the back door. So what, if God knows, let the whole world know. Well, your defenders have started coming out of the woodwork here, this explains why for the longest time you haven't been seen with anybody. The fact is, it was a difficult decision and that's why I don't plan to kick off a romance until summer, and since you're on my list I promise you can be my first date. No way, that would bring seven years' bad luck, listen, did you take a look at the stuff you asked me for about Canizales' sedan? no question they moved it the night of the crime, the dead bugs on the front grille are a giveaway, then there's the dirty windshield and the tollbooth receipts. The guy went to Mazatlán before he died, we found the other pair of shoes in the hotel. But we also found a few guasachiata butterflies and they live in the north around Guamúchil, which means maybe he also went there. He was probably saying his goodbyes. Are we holding anybody? No-one, I'd like the techies to go over room seventeen of Hotel La Siesta, it's in Olas Altas. Did they stay there? Yup, how vulgar can you get. Vulgar, why? That's where Jack Kerouac stayed. Who's he? A famous highway patrolman from Massachusetts. Hotel rooms are home territory for Jack the Ripper. Still, we're going to put the screws on the dancer. What's your theory, Lefty? Canizales finished his shift at Social Security at six and left for Mazatlán, according to the tollbooth receipt he went through at 6.43, he got to the hotel after nine, waited for Aldana, they fucked until eleven or twelve and he came back, he went through the tollbooth at 1.42 in the morning; before he made it home he picked up somebody who didn't know what to do with a silver bullet. Did you find out anything from Tucson? A useless list of notables. O.K., I'm going to send Canizales' prints over to the boys in Mazatlán by email and I'll ask them to dust that room, I'll keep you posted. Perfect, he said, then admitted, though I've still got a feeling Aldana wasn't the one. Why? I wish I knew, maybe he came to see him, they fought, and he did kill him, was he lying when he said he had never fired a gun? what about the silver bullets? was he cold-blooded enough? even so, if you're asking whether I'm going to throw him in the slammer, yes I am, for being a crybaby. Lefty, what's up with Memo's book? I've got it in the car, in an hour and a half I'll give it to you. I'm a witness. Did you find out anything about the perfume? We took a look, but we couldn't pin it down, it probably faded. A few days ago I sent a sample to L.H., we'll see what he comes up with. That guy's crazy. But he has the nose of a Belgian shepherd. If he can't find it he'll make something up, is it true he resigned from the police to open a teahouse? Negative.

He was crossing Morelos Bridge when Shorty Abitia called: My man Lefty, how's the fuse. It's burning, Shorty my man, what's up. Here's a bit of info on the thing you asked me about, what's today's password? Z-47. O.K., there's a Colombian named Estanislao Contreras who brought silver bullets into the country, it seems they were made in Indonesia, he spent a few days at the San Marcos, but then he vanished, he didn't pay the bill or pick up his luggage. Lefty turned left at the botanical gardens, that's great, Shorty, got it, I'll be looking for you so we can knock each other around. You know I'll be ready for you, Lefty, and if you ever need urine, don't forget I have the best samples in the region. You bet.

Pink pants and blouse a lighter pink. Laura Frías arrived ten minutes late. Mendieta, sipping an espresso, showed the scars of the previous night. You don't look well, commander, you're probably trying to do yourself in and it's working, she smiled. There is nothing I desire as intensely as the end of this life. What, did andropause catch up with you and now you're on testosterone? More or less. Have you found the culprit? Not yet, we want to make him suffer, would you like some breakfast? Just orange juice. So you've decided to pressure me. Figueroa got us together yesterday, but I don't think people care that much, the fact is people go on with their lives and not all of them were friends of Bruno's, he was so liberated they were suspicious of him and maybe some of them felt envious. Tell Figueroa it's going well, we have seven detainees and we'll have a confessed murderer before you know it. Is that true? No, but it will put them at ease. They brought the juice and Rudy sent them oatmeal cookies. Let's see, let's try to pick up where we left off, for you the culprit is Paola Rodríguez. I've been thinking about Samantha Valdés' lover. Why not her father? If he wanted to kill him he would have done it without any fuss and probably he would have trumpeted it all over the place. Your friend was killed with a silver bullet. No kidding, Bruno always said if they were going to kill him, it should be with a silver bullet. Aha, which means the murderer knew him well and knew about that wish, but why would he want to please him? Out of love, have you thought about Frank Aldana? We went to see him in Mazatlán and he ran away, but we'll catch him soon, one of the best hounds is on his trail. I can hardly believe it, such a sweet kid, do you think it was him? I have only my feelings to go on, for the moment I've ruled out Paola, since she killed herself with a Beretta and Canizales was done in with a Smith & Wesson; the Beretta belonged to Paola's father, I've got the permit, how did Canizales meet Samantha? She was his client and she started wearing really short skirts, Bruno didn't need much encouragement, he fell right in. What about Mariana Kelly? The only thing I know is what I told you, that she threatened him, I don't know if she uses silver bullets, but she is certainly a woman with connections, she's worked for the government and private companies, she's a publicist.

Cavalry charge. Mission accomplished. Good, interrogate her while I'm on my way over. She says she has nothing to declare and she wants a lawyer. Give her a Diet Coke and tell her to make do with that.

Why don't you suspect anyone from the U.S.B.? I don't think anyone there has the guts, we're pacifists and we hate weapons. But they haven't lost their aggressiveness, you know Hitler ate salad for breakfast and liquidated Jews like crazy. It could be. Besides, who's to say he didn't touch somebody's sore spot. It's possible, though I never heard about anything, all his escapades were on the outside. How's your work going? Well, I've got four patients today, as a matter of fact the first is in twenty minutes, two blocks away; last night Zelda turned up at my house, why didn't you come? I had to be somewhere else, and speaking of that, Zelda was impressed with Bruno's wardrobe, why didn't you mention that before? Out of shame, I suppose, or maybe prejudice, I thought it would be wrong if you held that against him, maybe you would take the case more seriously if you thought he was macho. Did he tell you about the conversation with his father about him running for office? Yes, some people are promoting him as a substitute for his party's candidate and he didn't want that ruined by Bruno's carousing and exhibitionism. Why don't you suspect the father? How could you think such a thing, that's going too far. Do you think political power is no big deal? But going that far? His mother said no buts about it, the father had him killed. Really? her face darkened, but she did not say a word. What's wrong? Bruno never wanted to tell me about it, he only made jokes about how politics had dislocated his father's feelings. Silence. I've got to go, are you going to want a massage or not? Of course I want one, except I'm like a hunk of bread dough: I'm half dead. You're really tense. It's the hangover, do you have any relationship with Bruno's parents? None at all, he hardly ever visited them. Why did he play the drag queen? He said it was the in thing, he had friends who did it, and it was fun. How do you know so much about your friend? I wish that were the case.

They said goodbye.

Mendieta. Noriega here, listen, that fucking dancer is a pro, he didn't leave a single clue worth following. Would you like me to send someone down to find him? since you people are worthless. Zelda Toledo would be welcome, we could use her instincts. It may be the dead man was in Mazatlán the night of the crime, he might have taken one of Aldana's shoes and left one of his own as a token of his love, his car is covered in bugs and the windshield is greasy. I haven't been much help, but I do have my good points and I expect to see that woman soon, I've dreamt about her three times already. I don't want you blaming me for your unhappiness, I'll send her down next week. Too bad for you if you're lying. How did it go on the high seas? Routine, we saw the water, we interrogated a few fishermen who knew nothing, and we came back.

He parked at the Forum, turned off his cell phone, and went in to watch "Brokeback Mountain". A favourite for the Oscar.

He looked over at the glass popcorn stand and gave it a wide berth, not feeling up to it. He started to go in, then came back: I can't possibly run away from that too, before Parra mentioned it I ate it with no problem, so what happened? I'm going to get a big tub, who cares if it tastes like nettles. He was sweating. While he waited in line he kept his hands in his pants pockets and his eyes on the posters.

He bought caramel popcorn, candied almonds, Coca-Cola and he sat down in the middle of the theatre. He relaxed: This is the life, not that pack of lunatics killing each other for ridiculous reasons like pocketing a few pesos or a few moments of love. Could Laura Frías have murdered her friend? I'll ask Zelda to look into it. Everything was going well, the music, the photography, until the moment the cowboys kissed. End of that. Popcorn on the floor. Urge to scream. Run. Die. Eight o'clock at night. It's eight, father, I have to go, I have to have supper with my mother. Bardominos hugged you, you felt his warm trembling body, you smelled his lust. My child, he spluttered, you are the sweetest, that's why I like to get close to you, you're also the best looking, the best behaved, and the smartest. And you were paralysed. And now you're dreaming of his disgusting smile, his hands pulling down your pants, touching your ass. He stood up abruptly, dumping his drink. People whistled and shouted. Bardominos had not bought him popcorn, he remembered now, or Coke or anything, but he had caressed his crotch.

He went out. He got into the Jetta, but did not turn the ignition. He saw he was falling once more into a bottomless pit, memories he thought he had under control were licking at him like flames. Parra had convinced him he could live with it, and he did for a few days without losing his cool, but now the abuse was choking him. Goga had given him back his dignity as a man, yet he reacted like this? What kind of guy was he? He had to give her her due: Goga, I never told you, thank you for making me feel like the greatest in the world, all those orgasms of yours gave me back my confidence as a lover even if you then ran off without saying goodbye, turning me to shit.

Later on, he was driving down the Valadés Parkway near Mariana Kelly's house and he felt tempted to find Goga: Goga you are the best thing that ever happened to me. On the verge of stopping, he accelerated. Better to let things lie.

Goga Fox: her absence had him by the balls, why did she agree to play along? Did Samantha Valdés bring her here as a way to make fun of him or did she come on her own? Life is so many things and no-one knows half of them. A minute later he was again overcome by the urge to find her, to stand in front of her and kiss her until their clothes slid off by themselves, but bitter memories stopped him. He felt the anguish of abandonment and he wanted to cry, why not? Fucking life. Like Gracián used to say, what can you expect if it starts with the screams of the mother giving birth and the wails of the lump being born. Best to steer clear of everything that has any relation to Goga, Blondie, as my friends used to call her.

He knew he had Mariana Kelly at Headquarters, but he wanted to make her suffer so she would know she was at a disadvantage, at the mercy of fate. So what if she had friends in government? Let her use them, let her call the governor or his chief of staff. He did not believe she was guilty, he still thought it was a man, some emotional cripple who could not stand being dumped by that degenerate Canizales and who used that particular fragrance. Was he dealing with a pro? He knew that track, a professional sticks to a certain way of doing things and that makes him easy to handle, but suppose he wasn't? Someone motivated by passion is a loose cannon. He turned up the volume on the stereo, "My Way" by Frank Sinatra.

He thought about Valdés, he ought to question him. He drove near Colinas de San Miguel, but desisted, and before reaching La Lomita he turned back.

It was quarter to four when he landed at Headquarters. Zelda was waiting for him. Commander Briseño let her go, she said, he treated me like the post in a chicken coop and ordered me not to move from here until you turned up; he's in his office. Strong sweet aroma. The roses basked on Mendieta's desk, top-heavy and resplendent. I told you to get rid of that garbage. Please, boss, don't chew me out, I can't face it, everyone here is nuts. We are, my dear, you are part of the team. Can I go eat? Just leave Ortega's report where I can find it, will Bruno's parents see us? The father left today for Mexico City, they couldn't tell me when he'd be back, the mother agreed to see us at seven in the morning. So early? It's when she takes a ride on her bicycle and she wants us to go with her. Seriously? Would I kid you? I hope not and I hope you like riding a bike. I don't, but I'll go along anyway. You should bring Figueroa in, the skinny guy from the U.S.B., give him a fright. O.K., but you'll have to deal with Human Rights. Did you talk with Rodríguez's night snoozeman? He confirmed that he left the office at 11.40 on Thursday. Good.

Evening, chief. What's wrong with you, Mendieta? are you your own boss or what, I've been waiting for you the whole fucking day, I didn't even go to lunch, and you don't show your face until now, are you working remotely or what? the Canizales case, I need the latest on it and no-one knows anything, you should have told me it was all a secret and I wouldn't bother you. Briseño was easygoing and could be funny, but when he got mad he fixed you with the glare of an enraged animal, too bad for whoever happened to be nearby. What's up with you, Lefty? would you like to guard the Headquarters door and bring us Cokes? is it too much to tell me where we are with Canizales, I want to know and I want to know now, he banged on the desk with his fist; the district attorney has been calling the whole goddamn day and I have not picked up the telephone or answered the cell because I'm sure that's what it's for, I have no desire to have my knuckles rapped on your account. Soon enough it came out: Quiroz had called him for a quote and he had no idea what to say; so on "Eyes on the Night" a string of wild statements were attributed to him and he was not going to let that lie. Over my dead body, he swore. On Briseño's desk sat three boxes of jumbo shrimp with a card he pulled off and hid from view. Chief, if you won't let me interrogate the principal suspect, what do you want me to report? you know about Paola Rodríguez killing herself with her father's Beretta, about Frank Aldana's escape, who by the way was spotted yesterday on Cerro Nevería in Mazatlán, about Samantha Valdés' temper; the U.S.B. is pressuring me and threatening to publish a paid ad accusing you if we don't get results, what more do you want?

You had Mariana Kelly waiting here all day long, what's wrong with you? So what, she's a suspect who ought to be interrogated, since when are we so considerate? the telephone rang. That's the district attorney. Well, tell him what we have, it'll be worse if you don't answer. Briseño picked up: Hello, he made a sign with his index finger that he had been right, I am listening, Señor District Attorney sir, he nodded a couple of times, said: Aha, aha, very well, whatever you wish, don't worry, of course, I understand perfectly. He hung up. He let himself fall against the chair back and closed his eyes, he made a theatrical gesture and turned towards the detective, jubilant: Lefty, you have a fucking luck I wish I had if only on Sundays, truly, I envy you. Chief, I'm a cop, what did you expect? You could be a taco-man or a bricklayer and it'd be the same story, you must have been born under a lucky star. With you for a customer I'd be rich. I'm telling you, you are so lucky you are about to close the case. Tell me about it. And on top of that you stepped on somebody's toes. I figured, he thought, then warned: And you know we've just started. They called from Mexico City, no matter how much we want to, we are not to set foot on Marcelo Valdés' territory, there are agreements at the top and we shouldn't ask for explanations; what do you make of that? Well, they're from Mexico City, what do you expect, they don't have a clue what happens anywhere except the capital, the feds blame us for being the most violent city in the country and meanwhile they cook up their deals and immobilise us. For the moment, could we make an exception? just wondering. You are the boss. But you are the detective. I'm not going to show Marcelo Valdés my backside. Don't take it that way, tell the people from the U.S.B. that we're investigating and then close the case, you're no dolt, and a good listener doesn't need many words. Next you'll scold me for sucking my thumb. Look, let's do ourselves a favour, since the case is bigger than us and you don't like the narcos, let's hand it over to Narcotics and that'll be the end of it, we call Pineda, we give him everything we have, and our problems disappear, agreed? Well, I repeat: You are the boss. Tomorrow stay in your office until Pineda's people show up and we'll be free of all this.

He left Headquarters wanting to laugh. Does Engineer Canizales really want him to continue investigating? Did he say it out of courtesy? Because all this has turned sour. He hardly had any savings, so no way could he resign and buy a house where no-one knew him to live out the rest of his days.

The lobby of the Hotel San Marcos was filled with well-dressed people attending a convention of criminal lawyers. He saw a few who were well known for their chicanery and he clung to one thought: You've gotta feed your face and get some ass 'cause this old world is gonna pass. Estanislao Contreras spent two nights here. The third, when the crime was committed, he did not return or pick up his things or pay his bill. They let him see a black suitcase with two changes of clothing, a Saint Jude medal, and a box of bullets, half full: lead. The hotel register had him coming from Tucson, Arizona, the land of silver bullets.

Cavalry charge. My copper, I can't make it, I'm caught in something with my brother-in-law and it's not going to finish soon, but don't whine, it's no big deal. When can we see each other? Tomorrow, same place, same time, and if they ask you why you're crying, tell them a piece of garbage fell in your eye.

He paused at El Quijote, but did not get out, two young men in Versace shirts, cowboy boots, and thick gold chains were keeping watch. A Hummer nearby. Am I up to no good? No. Nevertheless, he drove off. It just might be the devil; a bird on the fly is worth a hundred in hand.

He ended up at home facing a bottle of tequila and a cooler full of beer. Dr Parra? He can fuck himself, there are only a few ways of living your life and this is one of them. He put on oldies: Chicago's "Questions 67 and 68". Trudis had left him steak and potatoes that made his mouth water, he put a plate in the microwave, but he did not manage to take it out. Someone parked with barely a sound and turned out the lights. Noise at the gate. Bullets. Bullets flying. Bullets all over. Crouched down. Behind the bar in the kitchen. Windowpanes shattering. Noise. Door full of holes. Letting it rip. Silence. They were waiting on him. He knew his Beretta was worth shit, but he fired it anyway. Two automatic rifles emptied out their magazines. The ammo burst all over the living room, the dining room, and the stove. He fired his fifteen shots and waited.

A Ford Lobo drove quietly away. The Chicago song continued.

He stood up and called Briseño: Chief, could you send someone over, I just suffered an R-32 at my house. Are you O.K.? I'm not going to let myself get killed by those assholes.

A few neighbours came by, but Mendieta reassured them, told them to go back home. My man Lefty, whatever I can do for you, you know, you're from here and we aren't going to let them pump you full of lead no matter who it is. You just say the word, offered the most peaceful among them.

A few minutes later Zelda Toledo, Guillermo Ortega, and a couple of technicians arrived, along with two patrolmen. Boss, look at you, have you been to the bathroom? Twice, Zelda, go home to bed, there's no mystery here. Thank you, boss, are we going to Navolato? Why not? only you'll have to pick me up, the Jetta is really a mess. See you at six then. Sleep tight. The technicians picked up the shells and counted them: a hundred and two. Door torn to shreds, curtain in tatters, windows in shards and slivers. He pulled open the door of the car, which had its hindquarters pulverised, the trunk full of holes, and the back window in bits, he gave Ortega the copy of *Pedro Páramo*. You go get some rest too, they're A.K.-47 and it was probably Yoonohoo Valdés' people. Why do you say that? A little while ago I saw a stakeout at El Quijote that gave me a bad vibe and I decided not to go in; today we held Mariana Kelly for a few minutes, she's a suspect in the Canizales murder, and do you know what Briseño did? he begged her pardon and sent her home;

140

and that isn't all, tomorrow we're handing the case over to Narcotics, what do you think of that? He peed his pants. That's what I told him, tell Memo the book is a gift, tell him to start reading it and not stop, that's the only way he'll be less of a dummy than his dad. And his Uncle Lefty. See you tomorrow.

Twenty-Six

Chief Matías, how are you?

Very well, forgive me for calling at this late hour, but we miss you so, how is your mother? She's just fine, my goodness, chief, it's so nice of you to call, thank you. How are you managing with those violent state troopers? Fine, I adapted quickly, now we're working on a really interesting case, there are suspects, dead witnesses, disappeared people, and all that; a little while ago my boss suffered a brutal attack, they emptied two fully loaded A.K.s into his house.

Pretty risky for a sweet girl like you, don't you think? any day when you least expect it, God forbid, you could end up crippled for the rest of your life.

There is no free lunch, Chief Matías, you know that, but taking risks is exciting, thank you for being concerned about me, why are you calling so late?

I told you we miss you, we really need your spark here; besides saying hello and finding out how you are, I'm calling to offer you a post back here in the Traffic Department; I have the impression that someone as kind and well-educated as you isn't cut out for police work.

Oh my, chief, thank you so much, I truly appreciate it.

What do you think?

I'm not going to lie: I'm really touched by your words and I admit that sometimes I miss the atmosphere at Traffic, but I have to tell you I'm doing well here, my co-workers are respectful, and I'm learning a lot.

Over here with us, you are the teacher, doesn't that sound more interesting?

Of course.

Besides, allow me to let you in on something, before calling you I spoke with Commander Briseño and he assured me that he saw no reason why we shouldn't bring you back, I have the impression that they don't really want you there, while here we really need you, there are so many young children and elderly people who need assistance. A few minutes ago I told Rodolfo that you were coming back and he was very pleased, so gather your things, turn in your pistol and badge, and I'll expect you at my office at 10.00 a.m., because we've got work to do; to begin with, at eleven we're launching the new Roadway Orientation Programme and officials from all three branches of government will be there.

He hung up.

Zelda called Mendieta's cell phone, then his home number five times. No answer.

She felt sad, abandoned, misunderstood; she wanted to get as far away as possible from these hypocrites who had done such a good job of pretending to accept her, the rats.

As a matter of fact, that very afternoon, while waiting for her boyfriend, her period had started.

Twenty-Seven

Cell phone off. After five calls, the landline stopped ringing. I want solitude to destroy me.

For hours he resisted the urge to snort a line, shoot some junk, drop acid, or even just toke up. A man who is lonely is a victim, of whom? Of the flies, sudden winds, and those who are absent. My brother is far away and I have no other relatives; I can't say the guys at work are family, the bros from the neighbourhood are closer, they proved that long ago. I'm a drunk weighed down by memories, a poor idiot who fell in love with the wrong woman, and to fall in love is to dream, to imagine a future that rarely comes to pass. He smoked one cigarette after another, drank beer without going over the edge because it tasted like water, and listened to oldies all night long, at the moment The Byrds' cover of "Mr. Tambourine Man". Though he knew his enemies would not be back, every sound of a car unnerved him.

Near dawn, he fell asleep. The tranquiliser and the alcohol finally did their bit. Trudis woke him: Lefty, are you O.K.? how awful, I turn away for a moment and they nearly kill you, when did the bomb fall? the swine, they nearly knocked the house down, if you get a bonus you'll have to spend it on repairs, the good thing is nothing happened to you, did you at least kill any of them? because whoever did it deserves no less, can I clean up or is Señor Ortega going to come with his crew to look for clues? last night on "Eyes on the Night" Daniel Quiroz was singing your praises, saying your work was vitally important, that you had modernised the police force and who knows what else; the truth is he sounded like a brown-noser. Mendieta sat up. Listen, Lefty, did you wake up as the devil or what, come on, get undressed and take a shower while I make you your Nescafé and some eggs with a salsa of poblano chillies in olive oil so you can pull yourself together; that habit of yours of dressing in black I've never liked, you should try something else, pay attention to your horoscope. Only coffee, please Trudis, and yes, clean everything up, Ortega came last night. I can't send you out on an empty stomach, I've told you that before, would you prefer shrimp in hot sauce? because I can see you didn't spend last night reading. I'll be back later on for breakfast, for now just straighten things up; do you know if Zelda came by? she was supposed to come at six. If she came she didn't make a peep; Lefty, who do you think did it? I suspect every-body. That's like suspecting nobody. When I come back maybe I'll know who it was. It could be some woman you didn't want to woo. He smiled: Could be. They were interrupted by the landline, which Mendieta rarely answered. Should I pick up? Let it ring, and it rang three times, seventeen seconds apiece.

Before going to Headquarters he drove over to New Culiacán, a neighbourhood on a hill, to the office of Foreman Castelo, an old friend from grade school who had gone from being an urban guer-rilla to running a group of killers for hire that operated throughout the country with the utmost discretion and who was not doing badly at all. One night he had turned up at the house asking for an alibi, one of his men had taken down a major from the Federal Preventive Police then fled, and now they were after him. Mendieta protected him, convinced Briseño that not everything depends on the one lens you are looking through and that Argentine beef is not the best in the world. The chief used his connections in Mexico City and in return Castelo sent him packages of Sonora's best beef every week for three months, and that was the end of it. Since then, all the while pretending to hate giving Mendieta a hand, three times he had done it, complaining the whole time while drinking coffee laced with cinnamon out of a one-litre mug. In recompense, Mendieta made him a present of his file, a voluminous dossier 316 pages long.

I'm wondering what the fuck got you lost all the way over here, if I'd known how annoying you were going to be when you grew up I would have wrung your neck back in third grade and dumped you in the quarry, Galindo and Chema would have been delighted to help out. He had a little office at the back of a garage with a metal desk, two comfy chairs, a Virgin of Guadalupe on the wall, and a bust of the legendary bandit Malverde in the corner, the latter two festooned with flowers brought in fresh every day. Drinking coffee from a half-full mug, Mendieta told him the story. We aren't the only ones, you jerk-off, I've told you that before, and that fucking elegance of using silver bullets is not who we are, we're the street, we only use nickel-plated steel; I figure you get that, but like it or not that's the way it is. Who might go for that sort of thing? It sounds to me like the cream, you know the rich are nuts; we get more and more requests for services where they want the target cut to pieces, drawn and quartered, castrated, what is that all about, our company is an ethical firm, we would never accept those contracts, it's a human being we're going to kill not a wild animal; but, like I say, there are quite a few of us. Did Hildegardo Canizales ever hire you? Don't ask me that sort of question, don't be a bastard. Did I let you copy my weekly quiz or didn't I? And now what do you expect, pain-in-the-ass? I expect you to make a few calls and then call me, my number is on this card.

He turned on the cell phone and it rang, he saw it was Commander Briseño and did not answer, there were seven missed calls and six were from him. Only you could have such a folkloric ringtone. Only I have the balls. Agreed, my child. Foreman my buddy, I need a big favour. Another? listen asshole I'm not your father, you're big enough now to stand on your own two feet. I've got Yoonohoo Valdés on my tail, last night he sent me a warning of 102 slugs from an A.K. What a waste, for any of my boys one would have been enough and you wouldn't be here bothering me. Lend me your bulletproof car. Castelo smiled: How do you know I have one? Because you aren't stupid. I can't let you have it for long, it's vital equipment for the job. It'll only be for a few days, if you need it give me a shout. What about the heap you came in? They ruined it last night, send it to one of your friends who can fix it up fast. Absolutely, start thinking about what you're going to give me on Father's Day.

It was a blue Beemer, totally armour-plated.

His bulletproof vest, however, was English. This is real protection, he thought, as he drove by two Hummers parked at a seafood place where the drivers were curing their hangovers. In the stereo he found Santana's twenty greatest hits, stupendous for cheering up any morning.

Cavalry charge. He made sure it was not Briseño. Mendieta. A 7-27 on Maquío Clouthier Boulevard, very near Ernesto Millán Park. Got it, send Zelda Toledo over.

147

Twenty-Eight

The kid with the bike left home early for the job his brother-in-law had given him the night before. It was his first day and he did not want to be late. What made a young man who had been a flake for all of his twenty-three years get a job? Radical change, he was even thinking of registering at Monterrey Tech like his father once insisted: If you are going to study, do it at a school that's worth the effort, Tech or nothing. That is why he had called the detective. He would tell him his incredible story. Besides, he had decided to marry Beatriz Rodríguez, he was still in love with Paola, but there was no fixing that, Paola was dead and Beatriz was pregnant. Beatriz wanted to have an abortion and run away under the pretext of studying acting, but he was not about to allow that, he would support her, of course he would support her, no way he would behave like a skunk, he would treat her as if she were Paola, who had never stopped putting him down for his negligible schooling and his horrible taste. He did not care what Señor Rodríguez thought and he hoped the mother would end up accepting him, well, wasn't that the story for most people? including his sister and brother-in-law, who also ate their sandwiches before recess. He pedalled along happily, it was the right decision and maybe it was time for him to settle down: The Mandrake is dying to occupy my post in the gang, let the jerk get started, let him move up, it will take him time to become the biggest ballbuster. When a man loses the love of his life it is time to begin another story, stupid as it may be, and that was what he was doing;

he was afraid of becoming obsessed with the dead woman and he would do whatever was necessary to keep that from happening. The book he had inherited seemed to get thicker and more complicated every day, to the point where he almost agreed with the detective. He recalled how more than once he had thought about killing Bruno Canizales. Yet things were better the way they were, maybe sadness would have killed her even sooner and he would have ended up lost or in purgatory; for now, he would be satisfied with the sister, even if she was not as pretty she was certainly appetising. A woman who is not beautiful is nothing, he thought as he pedalled vigorously up a hill on Clouthier Boulevard.

He was breathing hard when an S.U.V. with tinted windows pulled alongside him, the passenger window open. He recognised the driver and he made a face that froze the instant he received the bullet in the head and fell to the pavement, softly because he had slowed down.

Empty street. Although Culiacán is a city of more than a million inhabitants, many women sweep the street in front of their houses every morning. This time they were not yet out.

The S.U.V. vanished towards the Coast Highway.

Twenty-Nine

Nine in the morning. Mendieta and Quiroz arrived at the same time at the scene of the crime. Anything to declare, my man Lefty? The victim lost his life because his head got smashed in by a meteor from Saturn, who we are now interrogating. One day I'm going to publish all the inanities you say. You must want to spend the rest of your life crossing days off the calendar and eating beans with bones on Sunday, would you dare? Try me, Lefty, confirm a rumour for me, is it true they shot up your house, I was on my way there when I heard about this. Who told you? Javier Valdés from *Riodoce*. Negative, that fucking fatass has always been a blowhard, he spends his life sitting in Los Portales watching the asses of the babes going by and setting the world straight; you should hear him talk about people from Guamúchil, his home town. Don't forget that I owe you one, so ask and ye shall receive; listen, what's up with my girlfriend, I don't see her. It was true, Zelda Toledo was nowhere to be seen, what happened? wouldn't they tell her like he asked? He called her cell phone. It was turned off.

The technicians had blocked off the area, which given the quantity of spectators seemed like a Tigres del Norte concert. Who said I hate bands named for wild animals? At first glance he knew who it was. There is nothing impossible about this, he grumbled; he called Montaño, who was at a motel with a medical student who wanted to do her practicum with the police. One of his interns was taking notes for the time being, but the techies would not let him work.

Later on they'll make a fucking stink. Mendieta observed the look on the kid's face and had a feeling there was a message there, what was he going to tell him that night? But he was incapable of deciphering it. Evidently, someone else knew he knew something. He took three photographs with his cell phone. Let's hope they don't turn out blurry.

At the door of the nearest house a woman was watching. How are you this morning? Surprised, listen, can't you stop all this violence? the politicians, the police, the soldiers I hear them all making promises, but every day there are more gangsta-wraps, everybody runs off at the mouth about ending the violence and it's nothing but parakeet spit, where is all this going to lead? look at what they did to that poor boy, what did he do wrong? Were you the one who called Headquarters? I'm not that crazy, they give you the runaround and you end up without even the bus fare to go make a statement, in this country justice is in the hands of criminals and as long as you people from the government whistle and look the other way that's how it's going to remain. When did you see the body? About seven, the one who saw him first was Artemisa, that fat girl with the flowery blouse and the long hair, she yelled to me to come out; she was the one who called. Did you hear anything? A gunshot, but since that's so common it never occurred to me they did it right in front of my house, and to such a young man, his poor mother. Did anyone in your family see anything? No-one, they all sleep soundly and my husband didn't come home to sleep. I wouldn't want to be in his shoes when he turns up. And who are you to say that? look asshole, don't you start in on my husband, you can only dream about being as good as a hair on his chest, this is his home and he can come and go whenever and at whatever time he pleases, that's why he has his old lady waiting for him, do you hear me? now get lost. Where was Zelda Toledo? He called again. Nothing. She would know how to deal with hysterical hags.

Señora Artemisa, were you the first to see the body? She was a young woman, slightly overweight, but with a pretty face. I was heating up water for Nescafé when I heard the gunshot, a loud noise, but sharp, I came out and saw the heap on the ground and red lights disappearing at the top of the street, more or less where that green house is. What kind of car? Well, it was more or less big, maybe a Ford or a Chevrolet, I don't know much about cars, I always wanted a Volkswagen, but you know they stopped making them, I went over and saw it was a boy on the ground with his bicycle; I know someone who works for the police, I looked for his number and kept calling until they answered. Who do you know? She smiled mischievously: Do I have to say? it's just that I'm bashful, you under-stand, right? The good thing is that you reported it. He wasn't the one who answered, I think he starts later. That's fine, you can tell me another time, did you see anyone go over to the body? On the contrary, they all gave it a wide berth, a man wanted to take the bicycle, but we screamed at him, me and Señora Emma, the one from across the street, have you spoken with her? she's boiling, poor woman, like water for chocolate, her husband is in heat and he didn't come home to sleep, it's been several nights already. Did anyone else approach you? No-one, look, on this block every man and woman works nights, the only one who works the day shift is Don Leopoldo, Doña Emma's husband, and as I said he hasn't come home. What do you do? I'm a social worker at Social Security, will you look who is coming now. Dr Montaño was getting out of his Honda. Ah, Mendieta said with a knowing smile. Don't tell him anything, eh, it would really embarrass me. Don't worry.

Montaño ignored the recommendations of the technicians and the notes of his assistant, he quickly checked the body, moved an arm, took its temperature, noted the hole in the cheek, and stood up. Mendieta was already by his side. You bastard, I thought he was some bigshot. You didn't warn me you would be busy, besides it wasn't me, she insisted I call you, she was dying to see you even at a distance. Montaño turned cautiously towards where Artemisa was standing: Holy Mary, that woman never grows old, we were together when I was doing my internship and you have no idea how much I owe her, she is a master teacher, a true enchantress of a woman; well, as far as the cadaver goes, he died three-and-a-half hours ago from a gunshot wound to the head, it went in his cheek and came out his left ear, rigor mortis is just setting in. This youngster was one of Paola Rodríguez's lovers and I'm certain his death has something to do with Canizales, I would like to know what kind of bullet killed him. Find that out from Ortega, now have some consideration, give me a chance to bounce a bit with this chick, would you look at that body, she's as tempting as ever and she wants more, the young woman was leaning on his car. At noon, O.K.? More than enough time.

Montaño went over to Artemisa and gave her a long hug.

Mendieta admired the joy in their faces and wished he had had a teacher like that. In truth he did have one, but he was not prepared to open any doors that involved Goga Fox. The testicle he was chewing on was bleeding blacker and blacker, but he was not about to seek her out even if it killed him.

The priest Bardominos passed briefly through his mind and Dr Parra's voice returned: Get going, detective, use your brain to evoke constructive emotions, cover your old wounds with new experiences so you can achieve some balance. A nutcase, who once met Erich Fromm and now smoked and drank as if his life depended on it. Why do I refuse to go back to him? Maybe because I have to get rid of Bardominos on my own.

He called Headquarters: Robles, is Agent Toledo around somewhere? Gee, I haven't seen her and you know how pleased my eyes are to find her, he transferred the call to the office. Chief Mendieta? Angelita had the news. She came in very early and took all her things, she left her badge and pistol on her desk. What's that about? Who knows, she looked absolutely crushed, so I didn't dare ask. Thank you, Angelita. Do you know what happened? Not a clue, do me a favour, get a patrol car to take you to her house and call me as soon as you learn something, give me Robles.

Robles, find me the telephone of Rodolfo Uzeta, Agent Toledo's boyfriend. Don't tell me she has a boyfriend, we already raffled her off here. Who won? Well, who else would it be, but my poor bones. I feel for you, when you have something call me on the cell phone.

He had to bring the news to the mother.

Beatriz was looking out of the window of Paola's old room, she must have had some premonition because she came over right away and understood instantly. The señora sat down for a moment, her eyes welling up, Beatriz put her arm around her, told her he was an exemplary son, and that God had reasons for everything He did.

Beatriz's face was distorted, red, sweaty; she called the boy's father at his office and passed the señora the telephone.

Beatriz was too upset to cry. She's the one, looking at Mendieta as she spoke, not even dead will she leave him in peace, the wretch, not even dead will she stop hogging everything, she didn't love him even a little, she only slept with him to aggravate me; my father is right when he says that misfortune never turns up alone, you know? the night before last I convinced him to let me be with him, he promised to go to work, to live a normal life; we talked a lot, he was drinking, but he was relaxed, he said he was going to take the most important step of his life. Where were you? In my room, even though it was practically midnight I couldn't sleep, you can understand that all of us in my family have our clocks out of whack. Did he tell you what sort of step it was? No, he only said that Troy was going to burn and that afterwards I probably wouldn't love him as much as I said; the truth is now I love him even more and I feel proud that I am going to have his child. Did he mention we were going to meet today? No, sometimes he would get mysterious.

The señora listened to the father's instructions, he assured her that he would take care of everything and asked to speak with the detective. With whom do I have the pleasure? soft, seductive voice, educated. Edgar Mendieta from the State Ministerial Police. Pleased to make your acquaintance, detective, we have heard great things about you, this is Alonso Barraza, I suppose you know who I am. Of course, sir, he was deputy district attorney for the state. Well, I do not want this to get out, that woman has two of my children and my wish is that it remain unknown, I hope that is sufficient explanation, give her the body and from here on in whatever I can do for you,

Mendieta, I repay favours well. What relationship did you have with your son? Horrible, he hated me, but even so I want everything to move smoothly, I don't know if you understand me. Absolutely, don't worry, he could tell Barraza knew nothing about his son, we'll do it just as you say.

Beatriz offered to go and find the boy's sister and to identify the body. The detective made two calls: one by mistake to Montaño, who did not answer, and the other to Ortega to see if they had located the bullet, but got no answer either. Dante, who was still working his Rubik's cube, offered to accompany Beatriz, who was incapable of taking the wheel, their mother was still unable to get out of bed, and Señor Rodríguez was at work. While Beatriz was getting ready, Mendieta chatted with Dante, the math student, twenty-one years old, thoughtful expression, red hair. How long does it take you to get each side the same colour? Time me, he moved his hands quickly and eighteen seconds later displayed the result. Wow, you are quick, what's the secret? There is no secret, it's just common sense and a little practice. Mendieta looked at him: Let's see, in the situation on your street, there have been two deaths within a few square metres within a few days, and one of them someone very close to you, what does your common sense tell you? Dante looked at him: The two of them were lovers and given the conditions you point out their deaths must be connected in some way, the probability is discouraging, but on target. What leads you to that conclusion? The precision of mathematics and the existence of similar cases, Romeo and Juliet for example, he kept turning the cube, they lived under threat in the same city at the same time; each case is a set, an equation, you have to define the specific fields and see where they coincide, Canizales could be one link, Beatriz is another, he said when he saw his sister approaching.

Cavalry charge. They gave him Rodo's telephone, and he called him immediately.

Have you tried her cell phone? Several times, Rodo my man, I don't understand what could have happened to her. What I know is that they sent her back to the Traffic Department, today she's launching a pedestrian orientation programme she's going to run, it seems strange you don't know about it. Sometimes the left hand doesn't know what the right is doing. They ought to be in the D.I.F. auditorium, the inaugural ceremony is at 11.30. Rodo my man, I thank you and you can certainly expect a birthday present.

What was going on? They close the Canizales case when it is at its hottest and then they steal his assistant, a woman he had brought over one day after she gave him a ticket even though he was a policeman, everything as the law dictated, then she even pulled over a narco-junior driving his Hummer as if he were on a racetrack, she managed to get him under control and deliver him to a couple of uniformed patrolmen. Bad luck? He was not about to take it lying down.

Once the body was identified, he headed over to the D.I.F., down Zapata Boulevard.

He got hold of Ortega: I want to know what sort of weapon killed Ezequiel Barraza, a 23-year-old kid now in the morgue but about to get picked up. He's the son of Yoonohoo Barraza, right? Why do you say that? Here everyone knows it. Are they tapping my phone, or what? Not yours, but certainly his, for security. O.K., so do me that favour. Listen, what's up with the guy who sent you flowers, did you give in? He hung up, he was not in the mood for jokes.

Cavalry charge. Boss, it was Angelita, her mother says she is back in Traffic. He thanked her. Filing into the D.I.F. auditorium were hundreds of children in school uniforms smelling sweet. He looked for the stage door and slipped in. Zelda Toledo in her traffic uniform was speaking with Chief Matías, a man of about sixty, fat, bald, his uniform impeccable. With them were other officials in civilian clothes and in uniform. Zelda remained silent, her face without makeup conveyed a certain angst, gaze unfocussed, lips dry. Mendieta could not resist: Señorita Toledo, I am placing you under arrest, he showed his badge, you will have to come with me, he grabbed her by the arm and took a step towards the exit. Matías grabbed Zelda by the other arm: You are not taking anyone anywhere, identify yourself or the party's over. The traffic cops present drew their guns; although Zelda had not recovered from the shock, her face relaxed, she even felt like smiling, she had not uttered a word, but she was enjoying the show. Put those pieces away or I'll piss on them, is this the sort of example you want to set for the children coming in? What do you know about examples, you're a scoundrel, a hooligan with a record as long as my arm, Chief Matías said, Agent Toledo will never return to the police force. She's not going to the police, I'm arresting her for dereliction of duty. Commander Briseño walked in accompanied by Deputy District Attorney Alonso Barraza, both were there to attend the inaugural ceremony. What's going on? they looked at each other for a moment. Put those guns away, the dep D.A. said. The detective went up to the two of them: Señor Deputy Barraza, I'm Edgar Mendieta, I don't know if you remember me.

Of course I remember you, he smiled, and I am very grateful, he twigged, must I repay you so soon? It seems that way. Briseño did not understand, but he played along. Just two things: I want Agent Toledo on my team, he pointed at Zelda, and I'd like to finish the Canizales case, it is probably connected to the death of your son Ezequiel. Briseño was just talking about you, why are you so hard to get hold of? Well, besides the two murders, an attack years ago that I barely survived, and another last night that practically destroyed my house, I guess it's because I like living the rowdy life. The deputy district attorney smiled. We can talk after the ceremony, Briseño intervened trying to shore up his authority, how does that sound, Attorney Barraza? Reincorporate the girl into the force immediately, Barraza said, and we'll take care of the other matter this afternoon, couldn't she stay for the ceremony? They were walking towards the presidium. I need her right now. Zelda had no idea what to do, Matías tried to pull her onstage, but Mendieta blocked him, the dep D.A. signalled and the chief let go. Mendieta took her by the arm and got her out of there. Why don't I get a say? how come no-one want to know what I think or where I want to be? do I look like an idiot or what? Let's have breakfast at the Miró and I'll listen to you all you like. Answer at least one of my questions. O.K., I only wanted to find out why you left us, but as soon as I saw your face I knew it wasn't your choice, he smiled. A Black Forest sandwich is not a bad idea with some good strong coffee. An extra shot for the lady, please. Boss, this time I'm paying, what's with the limo? It's no big deal, Agent Toledo, you know change is my routine.

Thirty

Laura Frías, wearing a white labcoat, put on New Age music and welcomed her first client: Don Pablo, how are you? have you eased up on the food the way I told you? I couldn't, Laurita, what I did manage was to start walking every day and I got rid of the warts on my back. What about the ones in your armpits? Next week, I promise. She asked him to strip to his underwear and lie on the table, face down. Let's see how you are doing, Don Pablo. She went right to it, spread massage oil on his back, and set to work. The man, as best he could, stretched his arm back to stroke her ass. Laura saw the avid hand, raised it, and twisted it as if that were part of the massage. The old man moaned with pleasure: it was a ritual that had enchanted him ever since he realised she would never agree to become his Shunammite. Then she put some elbow grease into the massage and the septuagenarian grew still, purring softly.

She was rubbing his shoulders when two men came in. Gentlemen, please wait in the waiting room, they drew their pistols, I'll be right with you, and put the guns to the heads of Don Pablo, paralysed, his mouth agape, and Laura, her eyes skipping wildly from one to the other. The boss says if you value your life you won't go around shooting off your mouth, something you said somewhere she didn't like; the other artfully caressed her behind. I'm going to let you in on something: we're fed up with making threats, even though our orders are just to scare you, next time someone is going to put a bullet in your head, get it? Laura nodded, speechless; the

160

talker waved the gun in her face, the other took his sweet time, long as he could, he was horny, then he shot up the tape-player and knocked over the oils. They left.

She sat down, deplored her cleansing tears, and absorbed a wave of sorrow she could not hold at bay: Bruno dear, I have to pray for you and take you white flowers, I have to think of you always and insist your murder not go unpunished. Who is their boss? the old man sitting up on the table observed her. What do you want to know for, Don Pablo. Remember, I was once a judge and people still owe me favours, I'm not saying I can do anything, but suppose I could? They are narcos, Don Pablo, very heavy people, owners of lives and livelihoods. Their style is unmistakable, but maybe they got their start when I was in my prime, if I don't know them I promise not to expose you, I know about these things. I guess so, right? what do I have to lose, their boss is Samantha, daughter of Marcelo Valdés. Well, you have picked quite an enemy, girl. Suppose I suggest we continue another day? Of course, you've had enough, is this Bruno the son of Engineer Canizales? And my best friend. They say he liked to dress up as a woman and give the prostitutes at the Izábal Market some competition. Lies, Don Pablo, nasty lies, I swear. Good, Laurita, let me know when you're ready to have me back.

Thirty-One

At the Miró, cell phones off and basking in Rudy's generosity, he received them with red snapper and shrimp tapas like my mother makes, they analysed the situation.

He told her about the kid with the bike, who the night of the murder had seen someone come out of Canizales' house and it wasn't Paola. So, we scratch her off? He nodded: Let's not forget that they took the case away from us, today I'm supposed to hand over everything I have to Moisés Pineda. You don't think it was Aldana either. I'm not entirely sure. That leaves us Mariana Kelly, Samantha, and her father. How did it go with Laura? I left you the information on your desk, under the pistol, she's from Guasave, a good family, graduated in psychology, been in the U.S.B. for five years, very close to Canizales, her friend Dania Estrada told me she often slept in the guest room at Bruno's house, she was something like his romantic aide-de-camp. That must be why she knows so much. They sat and thought. Laura thinks it was a crime of passion, Canizales wanted to die from a silver bullet and the killer indulged him, and I haven't ruled out a recent friendship, more silence, Aldana watches crime films, but that's not enough; all in all, the devil doesn't know where to stick his tail. Will you tell all this to Commander Pineda? He made a gesture of who knows, when in reality he knew he would not give up a single iota. They ate steadily. You look like you didn't sleep well. It's just that I'm starting to go through andropause and that gunfight undid something inside me. Did you go see Señora

Canizales? You were going to pick me up, remember? True, but the call from Chief Matías threw me off. Well, it wouldn't be wise now, let's get it into our heads that the case is closed, even though I'd love to know what else she has to say about the father, more coffee was poured. With all you eat, I can't understand why you don't put on weight. Me neither. Boss, is it true you were a narco? Mendieta stared at his half-eaten sandwich, why not give her a vote of confidence? After high school I drove three cars full of coke. To Nogales? To Yuma, it's worth more on the other side. And then? I backed off, I gave half the money to my mother and the rest I spent. What did you study? Spanish literature. Why? I liked to read. You are the first person I've ever met who likes to read, so why did you become a policeman? I can't even remember, what about you? I needed a job; listen, I've never seen you with a book.

Detective Mendieta, Rendón interrupted them. How are things, professor, how are you? he introduced Zelda Toledo; how is it going with your car, did you go see Señor Urrea? That's what I wanted to speak with you about, Urrea says he knows nothing about it, that his department has no report on it. You didn't report it? Of course I reported it, I guess they lost the paperwork; in any case the car turned up and the insurance company doesn't want to pay, what do you think I should do? Pick up your car and forget about the rest. That's what I thought, but it's a real clunker, a '93, and the truth is I would do better getting the insurance money. I understand, do the insurance people know it turned up? No, I don't think anybody knows, I found it in the Traffic Department lot, they want to charge me for the towing and a month of parking and I am not lying when I say they want more than the car is worth. Zelda spoke up: Go

163

to the lot and look for Rodolfo Uzeta, she wrote something on a paper napkin and folded it over, take him this, she handed it to him. You can believe it, professor, that's her fiancé. Then it will work better than a silver bullet. Mendieta looked at him: Hang on, teach, sit down, have a cup of coffee with us, and tell us what you know about silver bullets. I'd rather have a beer, I really don't know much, why did the Lone Ranger use silver bullets? Mendieta and Zelda looked at one another: No clue. Because they're faster than lead ones of course, there is the matter of the myth and that could be one reason, but they gave him a few thousandths of a second to save his skin in a shootout. What do you know about the ritual aspects? Rendón tasted his beer, you mean Friday nights, were-wolves, vampires, and all that? And their relationship with silver bullets. I would have to look into it. Could you do that? He finished his beer, let's meet here in a few days. Sunday at eleven, don't forget. And don't you be late. Rendón went back to his table where a Tecate awaited him.

Goga Fox, who had just walked in, came over, evidently intent on flirting. Her perfumed aura arrived with her, Edgar, can I have a word with you? Off-balance: Of course. I'm Goga Fox, she gave Zelda a peevish look, and I would like to speak with the man alone, are you a crossing guard? No, Mendieta answered, she's undercover. How interesting, she smoothed a wrinkle in his jersey. Zelda, who knew nothing of the romance but a lot about women, stood up and moved off. Rudy, well acquainted with Goga's tastes, for she had spent many mornings of her life at his tables gossiping with her friends, immediately sent over an Irish coffee. Edgar, she fluttered her eyelids, how have you been? you look like you had a bad night.

Wrong, I even dreamt about angels. What happened the other night was not normal, I didn't expect that reaction. Goga, nothing bores me more than explaining my reactions and any explanation for you would be superfluous of course, that was a horrible idea to send me flowers. I love you, Edgar, I know you haven't been happy, forgive me, my husband was pressuring me more and more, he was asking questions that would have given us away, so when he mentioned your name I chose to make my exit, is it that hard to understand? Because I understand it, I don't want to spoil the party. But don't be so drastic, I came to see you and I don't want to leave without being with you, she put some sugar in her coffee, I have a tender heart, too, believe it or not. They sighed. Give me one night with you, Edgar, she murmured, looking into his eyes, her hands on her breasts. Have you ever, for any reason, wanted to take off running? Well, that's how Mendieta felt, flat on the canvas, he wanted to tell her categorically no, but he could not find a way, so he simply said: I can't. Goga's smile was indifferent: As for Bruno Canizales, I'm on your side, I know sooner or later you will find the culprit; I don't know if one of those two girls is capable of killing, but Mariana was really mad at Canizales, she might have hired someone, I don't know, but what I know for sure is that she's frightened, they've been at the house in Altata since yesterday; I have the impression she wants to speak with you, to clear up whatever she can, it's Samantha who is against it, the least she says about you is that you are a good-for-nothing, she wants to humiliate you, she wants you to come to her on your knees and beg forgiveness. Mendieta observed her, listened to her voice while controlling the chaos inside caused by having that flowered skirt and black blouse within reach. Her perfume was so seductive. She recalled: I like how you take off my clothes, the way you grab my blouse and my skirt as if they were public enemy number one. Why was she telling him that? he was not going to ask. She pointed at Zelda, who was at the cash: Are you going with her? Yes. She's got lovely skin. We are going to get married. Alright, someone finally caught you. We'll see if she doesn't take off like the other one. I don't think so, she looks like she knows which way is up, she grew suddenly serious, she turned towards Zelda, who was utterly at ease talking with Rudy, she's either incredibly confident or she couldn't care less about you. How are things with you? Magnificent, he's at work all day and I go to museums, galleries, or the movies, what's incomprehensible, as you once told me, is that I am the architect of this strange and often unwanted fate; I'm on the verge of believing that you love only once and that everything else is a variation on the same theme, but empty of content; somehow I'm chained to us. He could resist no longer: If you care to know, you are not only the architect of your own fate, you're also the architect of mine.

A uniformed policeman came in: My man Lefty, Commander Briseño sent me for you and for Agent Toledo, he wants to know why you aren't answering your cell phones. Zelda came over. Call me, Goga said, and she handed him a perfumed card. Zelda, whom Rudy had brought up to date, behaved respectfully. Now on her feet, she kissed his cheek with ardent lips, he was tempted to tell her, on both like in Europe, but he had yet to emerge from his daze.

Thirty-Two

Marcelo Valdés was pacing in his garden and speaking on a cell phone. Below crouched Culiacán, poised to strike. Three guards stood alert, keeping a veiled eye on his movements. You have deceived me in the worst way, how could you dare associate yourself with an imbecile like the Gringo just to take me for a few pesos? don't you realise the harm you are doing to me, the harm you are doing to my organisation? why the cheap tricks to take me for a few miserable coins? I never denied you a thing, not before or after you were married; your husband was a dolt, that's why he got killed, I supported you both, and as a widow you've never lacked for anything; I don't understand you, Samantha, truly, and I'm growing tired of your foolishness, your lack of consideration. It's not the Gringo's fault, Pa, I forced him. If I hadn't known that, I would have sent him long ago to be with his father, may he rest in peace. They fell silent for a moment. What did you want the money for? I'm going to buy a yacht, I was short. What the hell do you want a yacht for? we're inland people, your mother was born here and I'm from Badiraguato. To keep an eye on your operations at sea, Pa, to make them more profitable. He interrupted her: Who gave you authorisation to do that? it's such an absurd idea, like the zoo I built so animals wouldn't be killed. Papa, you're sick, you can't handle everything, besides it's time I got directly involved, people covet our territory and they're taking potshots from all over. An airplane passed overhead, flying north. Papa, it is your organisation, like you just said, an organisation that ought to grow stronger every day. Let's not talk about this on the telephone, I'm putting half a million in your account right now as a gift from your mother. What about from you? A million, but in the child's account. You always have to win, don't you. Sincerely, I believe it is the other way around, this is not the first time I've asked you to behave, it's probably this sort of thing that's made me unwell. Don't exaggerate, Pa, it's not like you live in a rose garden. He looked at the flowers around him: Let's just leave it at that, take care, and enjoy the sea and the seafood. Wouldn't you just love a fish grilled to perfection? Regarding your possible direct participation, we'll see about that when you get back, and do not ever again tell me that I am sick. He ended the call. He thought a moment, then punched in a number: Go ahead with Ponce. He hung up again, and turned towards the city.

It was all lit up. What pests, people spend their lives criticising us, but do they ever live off of us; I turned this slum into something, I built entire neighbourhoods and created more jobs than any government; I will not let them forget that; this was a dusty village when I began and now look at how big it is; they are going to get me, I know, but before that happens I'm going to relieve them of that stupid policeman. He called again: Take down Mendieta, he said, and he hung up. His wife came out: My love, who do you suppose is on the line? Don Pablo Villavelázquez, she came over with a telephone in her hand.

Thirty-Three

As soon as they turned on their cell phones, she received a call from Rodo and he one from Ortega: Listen, jerk-off, I'm going to put somebody on who wants to curse your mother, he did not have time to say no. Lefty? Who's that speaking? Memo. Hey, Memo, what's up, how are you? I wanted to thank you for the book. Don't you still want it? Of course I do, thank you. Have you started reading it? I'm on page sixteen. And you don't get it, right? Well, no, but I'm still going to read it, so the teach won't fail me. Do right by the jerk, make it clear that nothing is going to keep you down. You bet, I'll put my father back on. See you later, buddy, and take care of yourself. Montaño's looking for you. What's that about? They gave him the body of young Barraza and Briseño shat all over him, but he stood his ground like the toughest of the tough. I'll have to buy him a few beers. You'd do better to get him a woman, he'd prefer it. I don't think that numbskull is lacking for women, he gets 365 fucks a year and on leap years he takes pride in not missing the 366th. He doesn't screw himself only because he can't reach. They say he can, but he doesn't like himself. Oh, I was forgetting, the bullet that killed Barraza is made of silver, 9mm, maybe shot from a Beretta. You don't say. You suspected as much, right? Well, yeah. Why? Dunno. Instinct is a tool that should never be neglected. That's what they tell you in the courses. Follow your nose, Lefty, it's about time you figured out what's up with these murders. Where did they find it? The lady across the street had it, Emma I think her name is, what a

169

skunk, she admitted she wanted to give it to her husband, but the guy just sneered at it, listen I'll see you later. Wait, do you know why the Lone Ranger only shot silver bullets? To match his horse, he hung up. We have a pattern, he murmured. Zelda, who was still chatting with Rodo, did not respond.

Briseño welcomed them with a smile.

Mendieta, two things, Señor Barraza explained to me about the young man who was turned over to the forensic doctor without my consent, don't worry about it, no problem, I like it when you follow orders I don't give; as far as continuing with the Canizales case, both the deputy district attorney and myself think things should stay as they are, so no sniffing around and I don't want any argument, take a few days' rest, the repairs to your house and car will be taken care of by the D.A.'s office; you gotta feed your face and cook a lot 'cause this old world is going to pot. But that leaves my fate hanging. What do you mean? The two murders and I form a trilogy, Ezequiel Barraza was also taken down with a silver bullet. It's some show-off, plenty of them around. Engineer Canizales will not be pleased to have the investigation suspended. Engineer Canizales is more concerned about the big chair than about his family, stop worrying, let the world keep turning, and when I call you, answer, asshole, if you don't want me to dock your pay.

Zelda, the case is closed, definitively, let's take a few days off, you can start Rodo's celebration today, I'm going somewhere to take a break. Are you serious? Of course, everything is in order. I don't get it. It's an impossible case, which soon no-one will remember, in our report, which no-one will read, we'll say that once again the powers that be weighed in. Angelita interrupted them from the doorway:

Lefty, Robles is asking for you. Tell him I'll see him on the way out, he picked up his Palm, made signs to Zelda that they should get going. Before leaving he turned, took the bouquet of flowers, and tossed it in the wastebasket without a petal dropping; even trashed, the flowers looked beautiful and significant.

Waiting for them with Robles was Frank Aldana.

Mendieta signalled to Zelda to take charge. Señorita, I did not kill him, I swear, I could never kill someone I loved, I ran because I was afraid, in this country falling into the hands of the police is the worst that could happen to anyone; Bruno was with me for a little while in Mazatlán Thursday night, we went out to eat and he headed back about 1.00 a.m.; you have no idea what an awful time I've had, but I can't stand it anymore, if you are going to arrest me, just do it, I'd rather be in jail than go on trying to hide. Zelda kicked him in the crotch, punched him in the face, grabbed him by the shirt: Get lost, asshole, I don't want to see you again in my life, ever, do you hear? if you cross my path again, for as long as you live, I will kick the shit out of you. She shoved him hard. Mystified, Aldana fled in a hurry. Robles could not shake his astonishment. So what's wrong with you? Nothing, Agent Toledo, nothing. They left. Once they were in the Beemer they laughed to their hearts' content.

He dropped her at the D.I.F., where she had left her car.

He turned on the radio: "So far this year, the State Human Rights Commission has recorded three cases in which police officers handed detained people over to private individuals so they would be 'disposed of', according to Commission President Óscar Loza Ochoa. The most recent of these documented cases occurred on January 19 of this year, at which time Professor Loza made the

171

following recommendation . . . Get the full story on 'Eyes on the Night'. This is Daniel Quiroz reporting."

He turned it off, fucking Quiroz, you keep biting the hand that feeds you.

Like a curse, the fragrance wafted out of his pocket. He pulled out the card, looked at the number, sniffed it. Fabulous. A stoplight held him up at Zapata and Bravo, among the jumble of road signs one pointed to the Col Pop and another to Ley Tres Ríos supermarket and its parking lot, which had been their meeting place. He took out his cell phone. Before anyone answered he hung up and turned towards his own neighbourhood. He was sweating. He was cursing. He was banging on the steering wheel. When he reached Santa Cruz he changed his mind, made a U-turn, and drove towards Tres Ríos. They were right when they said you don't need to study to become a bonehead.

Remember and die.

He turned in the direction of the Fiesta Inn, went under the Orabá Island bridge, and a minute later parked in the usual place. He saw the kid with the beret come out with a shopping cart and start unloading it into a Windstar van. He smiled. Without love, I am a piece of shit.

He answered a call from Laura, who told him about the assault. I'm scared stiff, commander. Do things the way you always do and don't let any strangers come close, I'll stop by. You can't come now? Impossible, I'll call tomorrow. He turned off the cell phone.

Forty-five minutes later, not having dared to make the move, convinced that he was doing the right thing, he drove home.

Goga Fox was there waiting for him. He turned on the cell

phone, hoping against hope for a call from God, from the devil, from anyone. Nothing but missed calls from her. She approached him smiling, white skirt, red blouse, the usual perfume, she got into the passenger seat. Did you call me? From the doorway Trudis waved, her smile between genial and aghast. Why don't we go to Altata, I'd love a ceviche at Gustavo's and while we're there you can have your chat with Mariana, if you like, he drank in her strong, aerobics-toned legs, we could also stay in the city, that is, if you don't have any commitments with the traffic cop. Without a word, he accelerated towards Zapata, one of the routes to the shore.

He who knows of romance will say nothing and simply understand. Sincerely, J. Solís.

Thirty-Four

Beatriz felt uneasy. She looked at the mother so in shock she lacked even the strength to cry, and she felt afraid, she touched her belly. What could the woman expect if she had two children with her former boss? A guy that Ezequiel cursed. Oh, why you? Ezequiel, tell me who did it, tell me why. I know it couldn't have been her, but I can't stop thinking it was; you claimed you loved her so much that nothing she did to offend you could hold you back, but you must have crossed a line. You had nothing but scorn for me, and I'm the one who adores you, it's like that Sor Juana sonnet I told you about at the recital: "The ingrate who leaves me, to be his lover I yearn; / the lover who cleaves to me, I, the ingrate, do spurn; / constantly I adore the one who my love ne'er returns; / I abhor the one in whom constant love for me burns." Is this the way it's always going to be?

She moved away from the señora to receive the condolences of her fellow actors and to chat a bit, everyone thought going to Mexico City to study would be fantastic. Any place but here. She began to relax. Then the Mandrake turned up at the head of the neighbourhood gang. There were thirteen of them, all wearing black T-shirts and torn jeans, several had dyed hair. One of them proceeded to scrawl "Zeke rules barrio 32" in big letters on the white wall of the room. Beatriz asked the funeral home employees not to be alarmed, to include the clean-up in the charges. My girl Betty, the Mandrake said firmly, my man Zeke rules, no-one comes close, I want you to know we are truly bummed out and we are gonna find the dope that did him, we went to the place where he went down and no-one saw nothing, only that they whacked him with a silver bullet. They told you that? You know I got my connects and, well, whatever we can do for you, just say the word.

Thirty-six minutes later, she called Mendieta and told him. Detective, what do you make of that, it's not as if he were a werewolf, she could hear shrieks of terror, what was that? Beatriz, thank you for calling, right now I have to break up a fight, I'll look for you later at the funeral home. But are you alright? Absolutely, I dropped in on Gori Hortigosa is all, a very dear friend, but he's still working.

Abelardo Rodríguez was drinking from a small silver-plated flask. Beatriz brought him coffee. Drink this instead, Papa, so you can last until tonight. Thank you, daughter, if you need anything, all you need to do is ask. The Mandrake just told me he was killed with a silver bullet, same as Attorney Canizales. Misfortune never turns up alone, daughter, it's a divine law. I suppose so, will Mama come? I don't think so, she's been crying as if it were her own son, but she can't get out of bed; Dante is outside with his friends. I saw him.

She sat down again next to the mother, looked long and hard at her frozen features: Cry, señora, it will do you good. The woman turned to look at her: No, my child, I've already done my share of the crying, the rest is his father's job and I'm not going to do it for him, she pressed her lips together.

They hugged.

Thirty-Five

He was about to turn off the cell phone when Foreman Castelo called: I just heard about your house on "Eyes on the Night", you moron, too bad they didn't kill you, right now we'd be taking it easy, drinking coffee, telling jokes, and your bosses would be drooling, saying what a good cop you were, how we have to put an end to the violence and then the big cheese would start in . . . I told you when you lent me the car, didn't you believe me? I thought you were exaggerating, now they say they dug out ninety-six slugs, you must have been shitting yourself, right? There were 102, do you mind if I call you back in a little while, I'm in the middle of an M-26. You just blew it, don't you want to know what you asked me? That's why I always liked you, I'm listening. You didn't even remember, right, asshole? you have your head full of shit just like everyone else. Spill it, I'm about to go into a meeting with my boss. Estanislao Quevedo was staying at the Hotel San Marcos, he came to do a little job for Yoonohoo Valdés, it seems afterwards they put him down and dumped him gangsta-wrapped in Piggyback, it all happened a few days ago, that's it. Anything on the silver bullets? They tell me he would meet the clients' specifications. Thank you, Foreman my man, I'll bring you your rust-bucket later. You wish, asshole, and take care you don't end up with a few grams of silver in your head, I heard they knocked somebody off on Clouthier. You know how easily the bros get riled. Don't forget my present on Father's Day.

Estanislao Quevedo or Contreras is a name of some distinction, maybe he's the one we saw in Piggyback.

Are you making progress on the case? the monument to Zapata receded behind them. It just got suspended. Why? I'm not sure, maybe Marcelo Valdés or some other big fish was behind it; if you think the police are keeping an eye on things, think again, it's them who keep an eye on us to make sure we don't step out of bounds, we have to walk a narrow line; Bruno Canizales turned out to be one of those impossible cases. Which if I remember correctly are your favourites. That's right, the line that keeps us afloat is so strict that the moment your attention wanders you go down, but since this case is impossible, nothing will happen. The murderer got away with it, she said kissing his cheek. More likely I got away, what have you been up to? Travelling, you know I'm crazy about those little towns in Europe, walking their narrow streets, the wine, the cafés, the darkness that never seems to fall. Why did you come looking for me? I didn't know anything about the Canizales murder, I told my girlfriends that I came to see you, that I didn't like the way we had parted, and I wanted to give you an explanation; bringing you to Mariana's house was Samantha's idea; those wicked girls, they told me about their run-in with you just before you arrived; I know Valdés was never poor, he was scrupulously careful with his wife's inheritance, why did he become a narco? That's a mystery. Or is it human weakness, "the more you have the more you want"? He's from Badiraguato. Do you think his birthplace matters? I don't know. Edgar, if I'm not mistaken, ever since we left your house that white Lobo has been following us, he realised he was so nervous he had not kept watch. Are you sure? Not really, but I think so. He could make out two men in dark glasses, he took his Beretta out of the glove compartment and put it between his legs. My God, she breathed, they were across from the Soriana supermarket on Zapata Boulevard, he slowed up a little, Goga dying of nerves kissed him on the cheek, the Lobo accelerated, and before they reached the traffic light at Manuel Clouthier, the co-pilot uncorked an A.K. and emptied the mag point blank, the bullets bounced off the windshield and the hood, all the other drivers floored it, Goga had crouched down and covered her head with her arms. If those idiots want to get killed we're going to have to give them a hand, Mendieta side-swiped them and they crashed into a concrete abutment, then he turned to Goga: Get out of here, take a taxi, once I get out of this I'll call you. Are you alright? Of course. I can stay, it's O.K. Do what I tell you. Then he called his team.

The killers managed to climb out of the pickup unhurt save for a few scrapes. Throw down your weapons, ordered the detective, taking cover behind the B.M.W., he saw the A.K. and two semi-automatic pistols issued exclusively to the army fall to the ground, he approached carefully, frisked them, and ordered them to squat on the asphalt. Buddy, you've been fingered and you're going down, no point resisting. Is that right? He kicked them, slapped them until they were bleeding from the head, nose, and mouth. Who hired you? Buddy, don't be a wiseass, a fuckload of the bros want to lay you out, you're not going to grow old, you can kill us if you like, but there's no way we'll tell you. Five minutes later Quiroz showed up, along with two ministerial police pickups, where they put the pair.

The journalist contemplated the operation, taking notes: My man Lefty, do you believe this is a follow-up to the attack on your house? If you really think you owe me something, don't put this shit out, Quiroz. My man Lefty, the public has a right to know. Well, they can go to college, search on the Internet, there are a lot of things more interesting than a fucking gunfight. Listen, I never saw you in this car before. Me neither. Before you go, they stopped talking to me about Canizales. When? Three days ago. That's why you brought out the stuff on Loza and the Human Rights Commission. More or less, who gave the order? Heaven. What are you going to do, the public has a right to know. Suck my thumb.

Fifty-two minutes later, after an intense session with Gorilla Hortigosa, a specialist in people who won't talk, they had confessed and were in the hospital: they were the same ones who had perpetrated the attack on the detective's house and had been hired by Ernesto Ponce, a former judicial policeman, better known as the Gringo for his white skin and blue eyes. The guy who washes the clothes, the detective reflected. He passed the information on to Briseño, who truly did not know how to proceed. I hope at least you'll make a call, Mendieta said, I mean, you're the one with the good relations. He left before the chief could utter a word.

He went into the Hotel San Marcos, sat at the bar, and tossed back two tequilas and three beers. What should I do? should I call her, go pick her up, or just forget her? She came to see me, is that a sign from God? Kids, you make such a nice couple, I want to see you together, you, leave that stupid guy you live with and go to him, he's the one I've picked out for you, and you, you shouldn't be alone, didn't I preach love? didn't I say love one another? you could even talk to each other about your problems, all that garbage you have in your heads. He saw her walking to the bathroom to wash, he saw her coming back refreshed, her hair pulled back, looking for the cigarettes. Remember when we both fell asleep? and when she turned on her cell phone she spluttered: My husband is going to kill me. It is so nerve-wracking not knowing what to do. Fucking unconscious, they nearly kill you and here you are stuck in the Bible. That's why we are the way we are.

The bar was half full. They interrupted a soccer match with a news bulletin from the local station. Mendieta asked for another tequila and another beer, not paying attention to anything.

You're a policeman, the bartender fixed him with a cold stare, you're the one on television beating up two young kids involved in a car crash, some guy filmed you from his car with his cell phone; will you people never change? will you ever show any respect for the people you arrest? will human rights ever enter your minds? those poor boys were practically massacred for a minor collision with a concrete post where nobody got hurt. He felt the urge to leap over the bar and kick the guy to pieces: Friend, let me give you a piece of advice, never stick your nose where it doesn't belong. This involves all of us, sir, Mexico is changing, even if you don't do your bit, there is more democracy today. Democracy my balls, give me the bill before I do something I shouldn't, he was giving off sparks. It's on the house. On the house of your whore of a mother, asshole, give me the bill or I'll bust your fucking ass.

He went out wishing it was into another life.

Thirty-Six

I don't get you, Goga, why is it so hard for you to leave him? it's as if you were married to him; I don't like that in a lot of women, they take a lover and it's as if the world had run out of men, they become blind, deaf and dumb. Well, with him I felt things I never could have felt with anyone else. But he's a jerk. Sweetheart, maybe that's why. Don't be a bitch, don't just agree with me; look there are more than enough men ready to whip it out; forget that idiot, he's nothing but a fucking godforsaken cop, I'm so glad you didn't bring him. We weren't going to your place. Forgive me, but I would have kicked him out the door, just looking at him brings on my period, I hope it was our people who tried to take him down, you would feel a lot better with that load off your back. Have you never thought how it affects me that you hate him so? Don't be ridiculous, I don't believe that imbecile matters to anyone, much less to you who has everything; you feel trapped because you don't take any initiative, girl, you live in Los Angeles, find yourself a black honey and you'll see how you wake up singing, a gunshot rang out followed by a howl from Luigi. What happened? Samantha looked out the window at the swimming pool and the beach beyond, deserted at that time of day, Goga, something happened outside. What? I don't know, I heard a shot and the dog whining, she saw Mariana running towards the house and she went out to meet her: Mariana, what's going on? A man shot at me and killed Luigi. Goga, they killed Luigi and Mariana's terrified, I have to go, we'll talk later. She hung up.

Mariana's heart was pounding: The dog was with me, I saw this guy approaching, I thought it was one of the guards, but he shot at me, poor Luigi. Rojas, Miguelillo, Samantha screamed, a boat sped away full throttle amid flying bullets. The guards ran to get their own boat, but Samantha stopped them. How many were they? One. And you all have colds or what? idiots, she went up to them and gave each a slap across the face. You give them a chance and it means shit, they simply don't want to do their jobs. She punched a number on the cell phone. Gringo, some numbskull tried to kill Mariana and did in her dog, he took off in a boat towards that strip of restaurants, see who you can call, oh, and the punks you gave me were worth shit, get rid of them and send me ones that know how to work. They were on the beach, Mariana caressed her dog, weeping, blood dripped from one of her hands. Then the pet stirred and tried to get up, his owner shrieked: Sam, the dog is alive, he must be wounded because I'm covered in blood. Let's find a vet. They raced to the green Hummer and roared off in search of help for the cocker spaniel.

Cell phone ring. Mariana, talk to Goga. What happened, are you O.K.? Yes, Goga, thank you, a bit shocked, Luigi's hurt, but he's alive, right now we're taking him to the vet in Navolato. That's a relief, let me know what happens, you scared me to death. Will do. She hung up. No doubt about it, Samantha said, that bitch is a good friend.

Leaving town, the women zipped around an S.U.V. with tinted windows. The driver recognised them, yet he continued on at a normal speed trailing the red taillights of the bodyguards' black Lobo.

Thirty-Seven

It was Saturday and Trudis had taken the day off. That night there was a Luis Miguel concert and she wanted to be well rested. You never know, I might run into him and I ought to look attractive, lively, ready to face the mystery of life. Agent Toledo had been occupied with her own affairs since the previous day. Mendieta had spent all of Friday at home with the cell phone off, trying not to think about Goga or the case. He spoke to no-one and read *News from the Empire*, which kept him up much of the night.

Although he slept badly, he got up late, put on Elton John's "Daniel", and made himself a Nescafé. Who had Ezequiel Barraza seen? and did that person know we were going to meet up? where did Ezequiel call me from? He realised that even if he was not going to pursue the case he was caught up in it, in its impossibility. Before deleting anything, he tried to decode what was on the Palm. Sunspots must have got to it, they say they damage the things you'd least expect, from a transistor radio in the countryside to a satellite tracking station: "silv bull, ritual?" A ritual with silver bullets? I meet Professor Rendón tomorrow and I promised not to be late; since I can't get this out of my mind, let me think a bit, every crime has an author, who would be the author of this one? We'll see what Rendón found out. He was going to put the Palm on the chest of drawers, but several numbers appeared on the screen. What's this? "Eng. Canizal", it read in his own horrible handwriting. Engineer Canizales' number. Should I let him know? Just to be a nuisance he called, two minutes later he had the man himself on the telephone. How did it go in Mexico City? Really well, everyone busy, working hard; as a matter of fact my lawyer called your Headquarters this morning and no-one knew where you were and they wouldn't give him your cell phone number. Tell me. I want you to shelve the investigation into Bruno's murder, definitively, and if you don't mind I would rather not go into my reasons. Did they manage to convince you, too? None of that, detective, let's just say I have no interest in ruffling feathers. Don't worry, neither do I, in fact I was just calling to let you know that your son's case was closed by order of the district attorney's office, although your wife maintains that the culprit is you. I know, however that is irrelevant. Not when you are going for the big chair. Are you accusing me? I wouldn't dare, I'm only thinking about all that can happen in a passionate campaign, besides the case is closed. Then, we have nothing to speak about. Good luck, engineer, and don't forget you have my vote.

There's news: he hates to make waves; for sure he's afraid of Yoonohoo Valdés; poor guy, our poor luminaries, up to their necks in it.

He took out the notepad and found several entries, among them one about the strange perfume, L.H., he had forgot about him. He called and after twelve rings got an answer. Mendieta here, yearning for another drink at the Dandy of the South. Lefty, what are you up to? I'm savouring some delicious shrimp with lime and ground red chillies and a cold beer. Me, I'm having lobster with beans and I think we're tied. To each his paradise, my friend. I would add that I have open a bottle of Château Camou, a '94, which arrived yesterday from the Trigo Canyon. To each his extras. That means you accept the tie. How is Tijuana? Impressed with the exploits of my twelve-incher and his honourable twins. T. J. is impressed? Yeah, tell that to the girl of your eyes, my Magda says hello, she says you owe her that story about Malverde's Day. Didn't I already tell her, I was so drunk I can't remember. Listen, Lefty, before you bring it up, I haven't been able to check out the sample you sent me, work is raining down, including three from the other side, one from San Diego and two from San Bernadino, I'm going twenty hours a day. L., my man, don't worry, we just closed the case. Why's that? Oh, you know how it is, too much investment, we're in the middle of a horrible budget crunch, etc, so when you finish that nectar you're relishing toss the samples down the drain and that'll be that. But wasn't anyone caught? Not even a scapegoat. So I owe you one. Get hold of enough wine, I'll put up the lobster. And we'll get the beans from my mother. Which are the best in the world.

Laughter, the infallible remedy, sincerely, *Reader's Digest*.

Thirty-Eight

In the late afternoon a taxi delivered Goga to the house in the Col Pop. Over the telephone he had let her convince him to go with her to Navolato, where Luigi had been operated on after the veterinarian sobered up. The dog was in the recovery room.

They all met in the vestibule. Samantha confronted him: What are you doing here, unrecyclable garbage? Sam, please, I brought him, I practically had to beg him to come with me. Well, he came, now he can scram. How is the dog doing? Fine, they'll give him to us any minute now, the bullet broke a rib and never came out; according to the vet it's because he's so old, here it is in this piece of paper. Can I see it? Mendieta was asking Mariana. You aren't allowed to see anything here and if you don't get lost this very instant I'm going to have you thrown out. Samantha did not back down, but Mariana passed him the paper.

The bullet was silver.

It was probably the same guy who killed Bruno Canizales, he put the slug in his pocket. The women turned to look at him. Naturally his target wasn't the dog. We don't give a fuck about your conclusions, you two-bit hero. Sam, you and I are friends, please I beg you, a bit of tolerance. You must know by now the case is closed. You don't say, detective, I was getting to like being a suspect, I suppose you'll be able to make this one happy after all, though the truth is I don't know what she sees in you. Not that it matters to me, but it seems obvious that you are also on the murderer's list. Goga gave him a worried look, what kind of a case was this? Chief detective, you and your suspects can lick my you-know-what. He shot at me, Mariana whined, her voice full of fear, I watched him take aim at me. Did he say anything? Samantha was about to interrupt, but Goga put her arm around her. Nothing, I saw him walking towards me on the beach, when he was about eight metres away he pointed the gun at us and I heard the shot, I screamed, and he sprinted away because the boys came running. Was he young? I didn't manage to see, probably, because he ran really fast, then he got away in a speedboat. Long hair, short hair, bald? He had a baseball cap. Did you see the number on the boat? No, it was too far away. What about the bodyguards? Samantha ordered them back to Culiacán, but they're still outside. He turned to the two women with their arms still around each other: One thing, Señora Valdés, leave Laura Frías alone, there is no reason she should be the victim of your tantrums. Well then, she should shut her trap; she could not say more because Goga's hand was over her mouth.

It was getting dark.

The bodyguards, two guys about thirty years old, Versace shirts, gold chains, baseball caps, were leaning against their black dual-cab Lobo. They must buy them by the lot, the detective thought. We didn't see any numbers on the boat. I'd say he was young, he ran fast and he was good at handling that powerboat, the way it took off it must have had 360 horses on it. Yeah, he was heading towards the restaurants. At that moment the women came out, Samantha carrying Luigi, who had awakened from the anaesthesia and was letting himself be babied by his owner walking alongside. He perked up his ears and barked weakly, something the two women celebrated before they climbed into the Hummer and pulled away followed by the Lobo.

He recalled Dante, how did Mariana and her dog fit into his theory? what was it that made them stand out in the set of victims? I'm so glad they suspended the investigation. It would have driven me crazy.

They got into the Beemer, failing to notice that a few metres away sat the S.U.V. with tinted windows, the motor running but no driver in sight.

They were passing through San Pedro, Goga was aroused and kissed him on the ear. Her breath was hot. Lefty, Lefty Mendieta, do you want me to call you Lefty? No. Why not? her voice soft, fragile. You are the only woman who calls me by my name. O.K., she ran her tongue over his earlobe, I feel like a Goga-Cola. Mendieta was caught between two urges: on the one hand the resentment cooking his innards, on the other the vindication of a man about to win the battle. He put a hand on her warm thigh, she took it and very slowly drew it to her crotch. The B.M.W. slowed. To Lefty the highway looked like a Möbius strip. He never saw the S.U.V. with tinted windows that pulled alongside at the speed bumps near Aguaruto and paused a moment, perhaps to scrutinise them; even less did he notice when it pulled in front without signalling.

He had asked her once: Why do you always wash yourself there? They all wanted to know and she always had the same answer: I don't know, doesn't everyone? My world is small. I guess mine is too. It was the last time they had seen each other, afterwards he read on the Internet that it helped prevent uterine cancer.

She had not changed: the same moles, the same agitation, the same smouldering stride. He thought: What is it about sex that binds us so? what does it have that plugs into our brains and alters our most fundamental behaviour? how does it generate such need? I wouldn't want to know. It pains me to admit it, but I cannot be with anyone else, I can't even think about anyone else, I simply cannot. Parra was right, now I can even mention Bardominos without feeling trapped. Montaño must be from another planet, what else could explain him? Goga returned, the very same freshness, this time she did not smoke, she just hugged him, caressed his hair, and they fell asleep.

Finishing breakfast, he turned on the cell phone, he had nine missed calls, among them two from Montaño. I already heard Briseño's news, no need to worry, he understood it all. Lefty, you already know what I think, I didn't call you for that; I called to tell you that Ezequiel Barraza's semen matches what we found in Paola Rodríguez; that much I owed you and now you won't see my tail until tomorrow noon. Will you be O.K.? Oh yes, you have no idea.

He fell silent, meditating, Goga was having a second glass of orange juice. A table at the back of the Chuparrosa Enamorada. Beside them a flock of geese was swimming in the Rosales Canal. Is something wrong? They closed the case, but this pain-in-the-ass is solving itself. Tell me. I'd rather sing to you. Is everything alright, Edgar? Jorge Peraza served them more coffee. Couldn't be better, Jorge, thank you. Why haven't you touched the custard tarts, didn't you like them? I swear it's because she doesn't want to put on weight. O.K., but what about you? I'm showing solidarity.

When you solve a case, what do you feel? she took his hand.

A profound peace, something like a good night's sleep. That means now you're restless. Like a rabid dog. The murderer defeated you. Yes, it does become an elegant competition, but it wasn't him, outside factors intervened and kept me from continuing. Don Marcelo, Goga said. Yeah, the one I told you about, Marcelo Valdés and his monstrous empire. Now that they've attacked Mariana too, don't you think maybe they have nothing to do with it? It's possible, but I have information that the gunman hired by the Gringo, Yoono-hoo's operator, was in the city the same day that Bruno Canizales took his leave and the next day he turned up in Piggyback full of lead, and don't forget about the attack. What about Paola? I don't think so, she did herself in with a Beretta and Bruno was knocked off with a Smith & Wesson, and then there's the bit about the silver bullets, even the dog got one. Though it was meant for Mariana. Even so, I don't get it, why spend the money? maybe he's trying to be original. Could that be? Why not? If it was Don Marcelo, he's beaten you, but suppose it wasn't? We'll never know, unless he turns himself in. Or he finds you, just the day before yesterday he showed his face at the beach house in Altata, don't you think he's following you? Me? why? You're the ringleader. Let's get going, I have to see somebody at the Miró at eleven.

He left Goga at Mariana Kelly's house.

He called Quiroz: I heard you the other day, asshole, and the fact is I don't get you. My man Lefty, it's nothing against you, it wasn't even me; a friend asked me to do him a favour, it's that simple. Who? A guy from the U.S.B., besides I didn't mention any names. O.K., regarding the Canizales case, here's the scoop. They blocked you, I know, there are heavyweights involved and they would rather not make waves. Something like that. People are even saying Hildegardo Canizales has got the backing of Marcelo Valdés for his candidacy if it happens. They've always sailed in the same boat; you know what's so strange, I'm very close to catching the murderer, I think he's looking for me; we're mounting a media campaign to give him some notoriety and make him nervous so he'll make a mistake, the last thing he did was try to murder a respectable girl in Altata and ended up wounding her dog; you can run with this, just don't name the case, you can call him "the silver bullet murderer" or whatever you dream up. What was the name of the respectable girl? Yesenia Guadalupe Pereira Ortiz. You got it.

Rendón was drinking beer and reading Ricardo Piglia. I thought you were going to stand me up, professor. You're late like you always are. It's a cultural practice that I don't wish to abandon. It's underdevelopment internalised. Did you get your car back? That young man, Rodolfo I think his name is, took one look at the napkin and went and got it and he didn't even want a tip for a cold drink. I told you, that man would give his life for my partner, what have you got on silver bullets? I didn't find much, it's a widespread myth in Western culture, Pliny the Elder was the first to write about it, in that case it was a werewolf, now it includes werewolves and vampires, which are another myth of eternal youth. O.K. Being sensually and sexually magnetic, they project elegance, strength, and vitality; they fear silver's purity and its use goes back to 1767 when they fashioned a silver bullet out of Virgin Mary medallions to kill a werewolf in France. So it has to do with sexual appetite. It's closely linked, especially in the case of vampires. Does it include the use of exotic perfumes? I don't know, perhaps in the Orient where aromas are common in rituals. Why would someone kill two people with silver bullets in Culiacán? Look, detective, I'm from Mochis, he smiled. Mendieta was still mystified, but he thanked him just the same: Have a few more beers to my health, he made a sign to Rudy, it was a pleasure and thanks for the help.

Like I said, the case is solving itself.

Thirty-Nine

Monday began badly despite the breakfast of sliced tongue in green sauce served by Trudis, who had been kept at bay by Luis Miguel's bodyguards for the entire show. Can you believe it, Lefty? those assholes showed no respect, even for a miniskirt. Maybe they're faggots and wanted him all to themselves. That must be the case because they were as rude as could be; listen, the people from the D.A.'s office were here early, you were reading and I didn't want to interrupt you, did you see? they only replaced the glass, they said those were their orders, can you believe it? Are they coming back? Of course not.

He called Briseño at home. Great, Mendieta, this is something you would know, do you think eggs benedict should have ginger? would it add a little pizzazz to their solemnity? I don't think so. That is precisely what I told Adelina, but she doesn't want to understand, I'm going to put her on so she knows it isn't just me. Better not, chief, I'm calling to let you know the people from the district attorney's office only put in new windowpanes, they were told not to touch the rest. Let me call Attorney Barraza, but for sure they'll fix everything, don't worry about that, right now it's more important that you tell Adelina . . . He hung up. He picked up an envelope from the telephone table. It contained that month's bill.

Surprise.

Trudis, what's this? he gave her two printed pages, four thousand pesos, what does it mean all those calls to the same number? Four thousand? for what, if we barely use the telephone, you just use the cell. That's what I'm saying, this is a scam; however, something in her face made him insist: O.K., Trudis, do you know this number? Well, I'm not really sure, Lefty, would you like another Nescafé? You aren't sure? whose number is it. Well, I think it's Walter Machado's. Walter Machado? who called Walter Machado? Well . . . Trudis, don't tell me you believe in that crap. No, I don't believe in it, she was wiping her dry hands on her apron. So? It's just . . . You spent a fortune speaking with that guy who charges by the minute? If you want, take it from my wages bit by bit, just leave me enough to eat and to buy notebooks for the kiddies. You make me want to hand you over to Gori Hortigosa, why did you do that? Shall I tell you the truth? she flashed an innocent smile. You'd better or I'll lock you in the dungeon for three days. It's that I want to know who will be the father of my next child. Are you serious? Lefty, I still have my periods, he told me it would be a Luis or a Miguel, that's why I staked out Luis Miguel, I couldn't miss; on yesterday's news they said Miguel Ríos is coming next month, imagine that, the grandfather of rock; if you don't mind, at noon I want to go to sign up at the gym near Holy Cross church, I want to tone up this part, she touched her behind, you know, if it's firm, no man can resist; listen, how did it go with the blonde, she's a looker, isn't she? What I want to know is how we are going to pay for this. Can I tell you how? the guys from the D.A. brought you an envelope, I left it on your chest of drawers, they said your Christmas came early. Trudis, you are a disaster, truly. Are you accusing me of abusing your trust? He preferred to take refuge in his study. He read, he thought about Goga, and he smiled the whole time.

At noon he went out, he had to drop by Headquarters and he had to give Castelo back his car. His own was ready at the garage.

He left the bullet with Ortega, who guessed it had been shot by a Beretta, probably the same one that killed Ezequiel Barraza. Mendieta was so keyed up that he went straight to visit Beatriz, even though he knew it was useless, maybe the kid had told her something else. First he called Goga: How are you? Wanting more, Edgar, Mariana would like to tell you something. About? About someone who is hell bent on you finding him. Mariana is the key? just my luck. She thinks she saw the guy who shot at her outside the building. Uh-oh. We'll be home all day, without Samantha. It's a miracle she left you on your own. Her father is ill and she's upset. I understand.

"This time he had Señorita Jéssica Guadalupe Pereira Ortiz in his sights. The silver-bullet murderer perpetrated the attack on the crowded beach in Altata when the young woman was playing with her puppy; the police assure us they are closing in, the evidence indicates he is a man with serious limitations, to put it another way: he's a dumbbell who could not possibly hurt any more decent people. For 'Eyes on the Night,' this is Daniel Quiroz reporting."

Mariana: Yesterday afternoon Luigi was really antsy, I know he can't go for a walk, but it was the usual time; I hate it when he gives me that suffering look as if I were betraying him, so I took him out, just to the door of the building, and I saw the guy, hands in his pants pockets, leaning against a green S.U.V. with tinted windows, he stared right at me and I felt a chill down my spine, Luigi started barking and he wouldn't stop until we were back inside the apartment, I looked out the window and he was gone. How can you be so sure? I don't know, we women always know. Feminine intuition, Goga agreed. It was also the look he gave me, filled with repulsion, concentrated hate; I don't know, the fact is he scared me. Yesterday you said he was young. Yes, from the way he ran, but now I see he's a full-grown man, muscular, wearing a baseball cap, tall, yes, more or less like you, thin too. What can you tell me about the S.U.V.? Olive green, like a Cherokee, I didn't see more, I was scared to death and I rushed to the elevator with the dog, he wouldn't stop barking. Maybe you're his next target, tell me about when you threatened Canizales. I threatened him all the time, every time I saw him with Samantha, I never understood why she wanted to see him and it made me furious when she'd leave me at home or show up at some ungodly hour all satisfied, and yes I asked the Gringo to take care of it, I gave him my savings, which by the way he kept; but Samantha's going to fix that and, knowing her, she will. Did you ever threaten Bruno Canizales in public? More than once, he always had girls with him, once it was the masseuse, what's her name? a couple of times that pretty girl who committed suicide, don't think I held back, I even let the girls have it, they wouldn't see the sun rise and all that. Why were you afraid to speak to me? Me, I never said anything like that, I've never been afraid of speaking with you, since I had nothing to do with it, the other day we didn't meet up because you were so late and I had things to do. What about the Gringo? Look, the Gringo gets moody, I think he's in love with Samantha, but I'm not worried because she isn't at all interested in him, on the other hand she was crazy about Canizales, in any case I'd like to see you try to lock him up, he's Don Marcelo's favourite. But you just said he took all your savings. That was about eight months ago; Goga, if you want, take the bedroom that looks onto the river, Samantha and the boy are going to stay at her parents' house and I'm going to sleep in the other room, I'll ask Puro Natural to send up some juice, salad, and sandwiches; after all, you gotta eat and you gotta kiss 'cause this old world is turnin' to piss. Luigi wagged his tail.

Mariana left them alone. Goga opened two beers and served the detective tequila. Something's missing, he said. Haven't I kissed you? No, he said kissing her, it's that you don't smell, did you just bathe? You could say that, would you like me to put on perfume? Later. What do you make of the guy? He downed the tequila in one gulp and drank half the beer: He's got a screw loose. He must not know the case is closed. Probably, or he doesn't care. Does anything indicate there might be more than one? Nothing. Does the evidence make you fairly sure? He thought about telling her how once he was sure of her love and that turned into a catastrophe, but his cell phone rang, it was Zelda Toledo begging forgiveness. Alright, but let this be the last time you make Monday into a saint.

There was a knock on the door; it was the food. Fruit juices in several flavours, salads, Del Rey sandwiches, and "ecological" quesadillas for everyone. They chatted like old friends and had fun watching Luigi eat lettuce dressed with Paul Newman's vinaigrette.

At six he said goodbye. He had to visit Beatriz. He called and the girl let him know she was heading into Mass just then, but in forty-five minutes she would available. Where are you? At San José church in Los Pinos.

He promised Goga he would return later that night.

Cavalry charge. Mendieta. I know that, dummy, you don't need to say that on your own cell. I like my name, what's up? Nothing, it was from the same pistol and if you will allow me I think you're right, the murderer is looking to get you in his sights. In your case, what would you do? You are a policeman, jerk-off, I wouldn't say the best but certainly the least moronic, and if you are enjoying this, well, get into it. Thanks, oh, I want you to use your influence to block all long-distance calls to fortune-tellers, salesmen, and tele-marketers from my home telephone. Even the Lovers' Hotline? You have that one all tied up. You bet.

Away from the door, the members of the gang were conferring in low voices. In the atrium the neighbourhood women were trad-ing recipes, old wives' tales, and praise for the kid with the bike. Abelardo Rodríguez and Dante, still clutching his cube, greeted him. The young man smiled: It looks like the only thing that brings us together is death, detective. Don't say that, Señor Rodríguez, how's business? O.K., this government has not been kind to us, investment in the construction industry is minimal, care for a drink? he pulled out his silver-plated flask, forgive me, just for today, soon we'll drink in proper glasses and in a proper place. Mendieta took a sip. Have you found the guy who killed Attorney Canizales? We are on the verge, the murderer, we know he is a man, left a visi-ble trail, he'll fall in a matter of hours. Well, congratulations, I'll stop thinking of the police as a band of muggers. There are two bands, one of them is good. The one you belong to, of course. Not at all, I'm on the other side and happy to be there. You're right, I can see you're totally relaxed, to your health; don't you get tense when a case is about to come together? What for, life is more than work. I heard on "Eyes on the Night" that you got attacked. It was nothing, just a wall torn to shreds, is Beatriz here? Rodríguez asked Dante to get his sister. She must be inside with Ezequiel's mother; listen, if you need anything to repair that wall, don't hesitate, I'm saying this as a friend.

Beatriz took him aside, something that did not please her father. He wants me to have an abortion, how could I do such a thing? it's all I have left of him, he told me that right during the wake and he keeps insisting, Papa can't think straight anymore; I'm afraid it's all that alcohol making him surly. Beatriz, forgive me, you said that Ezequiel was killed by a silver bullet, remember? He thought about telling her that the randy kid had slept with Paola just before her suicide, but he did not dare. Maybe it was the same person who killed Bruno Canizales, do you think they might have had a common enemy? I don't think so, Ezequiel detested Bruno, if he had been a bad person he would have killed him a long time ago, and if you want to know I'm not liking this one bit, what an awful ritual, his mama is seized up, she can't cry, can you believe that the father didn't even set foot in the funeral home? he probably won't come to the Mass either, the señora is so far gone not even the sun will thaw her. But you have your family by your side. What family? well, Dante yes, he's always there, as long as you don't take away his Rubik's cube he's no problem, my mother is with the señora, but my father just turned up and you can see what shape he's in; Mama thinks he's got another woman because he comes home with his shirts smudged, I think he can't find a way to get along without Paola. Ezequiel and I were going to talk the afternoon of the day he died, do you remember he said he was going to take a big step? I remember. Did he tell you anything else? he seemed to know who killed Canizales. Really? he didn't tell me anything, only that Troy would burn. You didn't ask for details? weren't you curious? To tell the truth, no, I was too upset. O.K., if you need anything, call me, say goodbye to your father for me, and help him out of that hole. Once I get out of my own.

Forty

In the small room, Marcelo Valdés closed his eyes. He had spent the entire day ruminating on the future. At his side, his wife flipped through fashion magazines. He drank from his mug of chamomile tea. When I became powerful I could not believe the feeling, it was a sensation I had never felt before, but it felt natural. It would come and go, come and go. I felt it in my chest. Thousands of men, it is a fact, stood to attention before me; telephone calls all day long and a receptionist or sometimes two answering that I was busy or I was with the president. Women. Great ones. Faking orgasms, saying they loved me, the ones that were not virgins confessing that no-one had ever done it like me. What an idiot I was to believe them for so many years. My father, before he died, told me to be careful: My son, if you are going to continue down this path, don't turn into a jackal, that would be hideous; but it was already too late. Have you heard about unarmed people getting mowed down? I ordered it. Police corruption? It was me and them: them thanks to their hunger wages and me because I wanted everything. We financed musical groups, political campaigns, relief programmes after hurricanes, fires, floods. My name was the name that came to everybody's mind. Marcelo Valdés is a man, not a piece of crap. How many corridos have been written about me? Enough to last the whole fiesta. And now. He felt a lump in his throat. We can't even deal with a miserable policeman, a bastard who hates me despite the fact that I had nothing to do with his misfortunes. A tear rolled down his left cheek. And Samantha so immature, daughter, you're so pretty, but so impulsive. Minerva came over. They embraced. When they told me that old men cried at nothing I never believed it, it's because we don't know how to avoid stepping in the shit. He hugged her tight. You'll sort it all out, I'm sure of that; just one thing, darling, don't leave anything to your enemies; and about that policeman, leave him alone, I'd rather have him around, he's a witless foe that offers a bit of counterweight, and he will never lock her up, they wouldn't let him. Then he gave up trying to hold back his sobs.

About twenty metres away, the bodyguards were smoking and talking quietly.

Forty-One

Bruno's sheets had smelled clean. If they really were, then who was taking him on? was it worth killing two people and threatening another just to challenge him? why? No way could Goga be right, that would be too perverse; of course he had put quite a few people behind bars, but he had never received any threats or heard that anyone was seeking vengeance; nevertheless, he was about to meet whoever it might be. Bad guys think they are not living their lives unless they are goading the police into action the way ducks egg on hunters. It is the awful truth. But I have to get free of this case, I've had enough; if I meet the culprit I'll say hello, How's the family? Listen, you were really good, always a block ahead of us. Quiroz annoys you? Don't pay any attention, he's nuts. Have you got any plans? And that will be it. Yet he went over the details once more: Canizales murdered, Paola's suicide, investigation held up, attack on my house, kid with the bike eliminated, attack on me, assault on Mariana Kelly, strange perfume, silver bullets, investigation suspended; and according to my girl the murderer is set on defeating me. Maybe he wants me there until the end.

List of those affected: Beatriz, her father Abelardo, his wife, the mother of the kid, Laura, Mariana, Samantha, Frank Aldana. Too many women. All of them except Mariana loved Bruno. The guys loved him too, especially Aldana, who Zelda Toledo exonerated without an interrogation. In Paola's case, only Abelardo and the kid loved her. The rest, to a greater or lesser degree, hated her guts. But

Paola killed herself. Who could kill someone that everybody loved? Well, they brought down Kennedy, Gandhi, Lennon, Colosio, Che, Socrates, Marilyn. It may not be a starting point, but it is a place to end up. From what Rendón found out, there was an overriding sexual motive for Bruno's murder, vengeance? There were no signs of violence to the body or in the room where the crime took place, pleasure? Perhaps, that may be why the murderer used perfume. Did Goga know Bruno? I don't think so, what about the kid? who did he see? Paola had his semen. Dante is part of the picture, would he kill Bruno and then the kid and still go around playing with his Rubik's cube? I'm so glad they suspended the case.

He observed Goga's body in profile, one leg bent.

Through the window a faint light filtered in.

On the fringe are the people from the U.S.B.: Ripalda, Figueroa, then there is Contreras, who both Foreman and Shorty linked to silver bullets, Gringo Ponce, the kid with the bike's gang, Mariana, Samantha, Yoonohoo Valdés. He recalled Foreman's report. Contreras was found gangsta-wrapped in Piggyback. Pineda could confirm that, that is, if no-one has greased his palm.

Goga had fallen asleep at least two hours ago, he was on his sixth cigarette when he heard a sound at the front door. Was Samantha back? What a pain, he would have to leave; so he cleared his head, but the sound was muffled and Samantha was rowdy, and this was her house and no way would she open the door so delicately, besides, whoever it was was already inside and had not turned on a light the way she would, she must be sleeping with her son.

He put on his jeans, the black T-shirt, he chambered a round and opened the door a crack. It squeaked. He did not know why, but a bar in Tijuana came to mind, La Bodega de Papel, and its owner singing a ballad.

He managed to make out a shadow moving cautiously. Mental image. He was wearing dark clothes. Baseball cap. At the squeak he hugged the wall. Mendieta tossed a shoe into the hallway and the shadow fired. Luigi barked in Mariana's room. The detective responded by pointing his own weapon. The intruder ran to the door and out of the apartment. After him. Behind Lefty came the two women, crouching low. Stairs. Lobby. Door. Luigi coming down too and without a bark. He reached the street to see a car heading off towards the Morelos Bridge.

He who seeks shall find, he thought, you are definitely not a narco.

Forty-Two

They were having breakfast.

At ten o'clock Goga's husband called. I'm so nervous, Mariana murmured when she passed her the cordless telephone; Luigi, eyes alight, wagged his tail. The man was at Pedro Infante Airport and loudly let it be known he wanted to have breakfast in Altata: I know how much you like the ceviche at La Güera's, my love, not to imply we need to recharge our batteries since we haven't seen each other in days, I just want to have something tasty at the seashore, did you rent a car? No, I've been taking taxis. So call one, turn on your cell phone, and we'll meet up in Bachigualato, where Airport Boulevard meets the highway to Navolato; I'm almost to the Budget counter, don't bathe, love, so you can do that sashay I like so much.

Goga wanted to die.

Everyone was watching Mendieta.

To top off the scene, at that moment Samantha came in with the child. Did this beautiful boy not go to school? We were late. Oh, César, Mariana exclaimed, they're going to give you a demerit. Of course they won't, Mama explained what we'll do, tomorrow I'll take a gift to the principal and another one to my teacher and they'll forget that I missed a day. Samantha noticed the detective: And what are you doing here, garbage-face? Who are you calling garbage-face? That one, what, don't you see his face? The boy smiled. Mariana moved her mouth, trying to tell her things were not right. Mendieta stood up and walked out.

Goga buried her head in her hands and was unable to say a word.

Poor Luigi.

There has got to be a way out of this besides alcohol, another dame, or writing ridiculous poems. There has got to be. He made out the boy screaming happily: Bye-bye, garbage-face.

Forty-Three

On Tuesday afternoon he returned the car to Castelo, to his home because he wanted to see him. He wanted to hear a man who counted on nothing and everything talk about a life without so much commotion. His sad bones ached for some of that pristine and unperturbed nonchalance. It was his bad luck that Foreman was not yet back from Altata, where he had gone for lunch with his family. So he sought refuge at home and drank half a bottle of Old Parr, wrote a Neruda poem, and convinced himself he had no-one to call. Not even the accursed image of the abuser made him cry: he no longer knew how. He turned on the television but the movies were awful, the politicians were spouting the same old crap, and the music videos were no distraction either. The Travel Channel was showing a documentary about paving stones in France that made him feel like the most miserable human being on earth. I'm fucked, he thought, if somehow I manage to get reborn I will never let this shit happen to me again, I've heard so many times that man is the only animal that will trip over the same stone twice and I simply never learn. Bardominos was back, his slender hands, his smell, his moist lips, his mentholated breath. He slugged another drink. I'll go find Dr Parra right now and he had better help me out of this shit once and for all, because by myself I just can't.

Telephone.

If it's her I'm going to hang up, she's got me hooked all over again, the witch, truly. Why do I accuse her if I'm to blame? The inveterate idiot has a name, it's Edgar Mendieta. Ring. Besides I don't love her, I don't like her short hair or her skirts or her perfume. Ring. She's so skinny it's pathetic, her tiny breasts, her stride . . . it's all pathetic. Ring. Hey, what are you doing at home, watering the plants or what? I'm saying the rosary. You used to do that with our mother, you were the only one who went along with it. You remember that? As if it were yesterday. It was a way to be with her when she was losing her faith. I understood that later on. You know what, I like it when you call, are you O.K.? You could say I'm struggling to control the urge to hightail it back down there; you sound strange, are you drunk? Me, drunk? bro, I'm a teetotaller. And my balls are square. I don't doubt it, since you're over there where science is so far ahead. You must have some powerful reasons to be drinking on a Tuesday and at this time of day. We closed a case and that was worth celebrating, we went out to eat, nothing out of the ordinary. How are my hometown girls? Those ungrateful bitches? up to their old tricks, you know they aren't any less than they ever were. Honestly, you sound like you're drunk. Not even tipsy. You're wasted, bro. Wasted? Enrique, it was only two bottles of tequila. Don't say the word, it makes my mouth water, besides which over here it costs an eye from your face. With the risk that it's made in China. Or worse. If you miss it so much, why don't you come for a visit? it seems like nobody remembers anything about you. Are you sure you want me? Of course. Would you take a few days off to hang around with me? I'm my own boss and I can take vacation. Oh, did you get a promotion? No way, I'm still a lousy detective without rank, some people call me commander, others lieutenant, yesterday a lady called me commissary. What does your badge say? Nothing, just detective. Well, that's what you are, listen I want to tell you something, don't get scared, I find it so extraordinary that I don't know where to begin. Uh-oh, what, did you turn faggot? Not at all, it's something else, nothing bad, bizarre but not bad, surprising. Spill it if you don't want my blood pressure to go over the top. Do you remember Susana, Doña Mary's daughter? Of course, Susy, I remember her well. She went out with you? We went on a couple of dates, I was in fourth year in Literature and she was in fifth in Administration. Well, you have a son. He took out a cigarette, what? He looks a shit-load like you. Eh, you're kidding, right? the doctors say my sperm can barely crawl so they're incapable of fertilising. Her egg probably saw they were dawdling and went out to meet them, who's to say? He put the cigarette away. I met him this morning and I couldn't believe it, I tell you he's the spitting image of you, he's seventeen and tall, national high school champ in the mile, what do you think of that? Amazing, like you say, it sobered me right up, he took the cigarette out again and lit it. I can hear that, in any case the dude wants to meet you, just like that, no commitments, what do you think? Mendieta took a deep drag: What's your advice? remember you're the elder. I say you should meet him, you've got nothing to lose, they live in Fresno, but they made a special trip to Portland so I could meet him and they asked me to make the connection. He took another drag: It seems unbelievable. That's exactly what I thought when I had him in front of me, wearing his black T-shirt and that innocuous smile that kills the girls without a word. In the street a pickup went by blasting a narcocorrido at full volume. When would it be? In the summer, Susana is going back for the first time to visit her family and the kid wants to take advantage of the trip, his name is Jason Mendieta. What? Just the way it sounds, life brings surprises, like Rubén Blades says. Well, O.K., give them my address and telephone for when they get here. Congratulations, bro, and enjoy it, not every day do you get news like that.

He turned on the stereo: "Reflections of My Life" by The Marmalade. He shaved slowly trying to recall details about Susana, but it got all mixed up with Goga, her sashay to the bathroom and her skirts. He took a shower and went to bed: proud Susana, a pretty mole over there, right? You kept that well hidden, didn't you, you hussy. Goga, go away, would you? it's over.

He slept poorly, but even so managed to pick up his car and arrive early at Headquarters.

Zelda came in with her Diet Coke: Where have you been, boss? aha, you shaved, wow, you look really young, congratulations, I can see you had a few days you won't forget, they send you flowers and you look like a T.V. star. What is this all about, Agent Toledo, I insist you show some respect and please, never let yourself be impressed by a shave. I'm sorry, it's just that you really do look good, you've shaken off a few years. Angelita interrupted: Robles on the phone, Zelda, did you check out the boss we have? That's what I'm telling him, he's turned into a metrosexual. More days like these, Lord, no. Toledo picked up the telephone: Homicide. A gangsta-wrap was reported on the Coast Highway, near the entrance to La Primavera development. Let Investigative Services know and Forensic Medicine, we'll head right over; boss, life goes on, shall we take your car or mine? Mine. The one that looks like a boat? no, it's horrible.

They were going by Ernesto Millán Park towards La Primavera

211

when Mendieta's cell phone rang. Please don't call me, even if you are on your knees, bawling and whatever, I am not going to answer, why is it so hard for you to understand? I don't love you, our affair is over and done with, and those flouncy skirts don't suit you. It was Carlos Alvarado, the only person he had talked to from the list of people who bought silver bullets. Hello. Sergeant Mendieta, how are you? how is life treating you? if I had not dedicated my life to farming I would have been a policeman, it's a way to be of direct service to society. I'm fine, Don Carlos, and you? A thought occurred to me, did you speak with my comadre Ernestina de Villegas? No, Don Carlos. I thought not, she was in the United States, her two eldest sons live there, she went to visit them, but she's home now, I told her you were planning to ask her about the silver bullets my compadre Federico bought, she said to drop by whenever you like, no need to call ahead; she also told me she knows where the bullets are and that if they are not where she thinks, then for sure they are at the farm. Thank you, Don Carlos, we will visit your comadre today, I appreciate it, goodbye.

I guess Canizales does not agree that his case should be closed by decree and it seems the murderer does not either. What do you plan to do? A little push wouldn't be a bad idea, don't you think? Is there something new? A few things. He told her what had happened, except for the strange encounter at Mariana's house. They suspended the conversation to listen to Quiroz insult the murderer in the name of the Federal Preventive Police. That guy is nuts, Zelda said, who would think of doing that? I would, he explained his strategy.

Moisés Pineda greeted them. What are you people doing here? this one is mine. Who is he? Felipe Garza, member of the Gulf

Cartel. What is he doing so far away? That is something we won't find out. Garza lay riddled with bullets in his Versace shirt and his ostrich-leather belt. To one side, the San Marcos blanket in which he had been wrapped. Captain, don't forget about our breakfast. The federal agent smiled happily, tomorrow at nine in the Chuparrosa Enamorada. That's a commitment, listen, captain, who did you give Estanislao Contreras' body to? or was it Quevedo? Pineda looked at him warily. Quiroz interrupted them: Commander Pineda, what can you tell us so far about today's victim? Lefty, ask me again tomorrow, he winked at him. They said goodbye.

They headed off towards Chapultepec where the Villegas family lived.

Lost in thought. Across from San Miguel Shopping Centre, Zelda Toledo turned to look directly at him.

Can I tell you something? the description of the S.U.V. that Kelly gave fits Abelardo Rodríguez's car, at least the one he was driving the day he brought us the permit for his pistol. Are you sure? The vending machine at Headquarters wasn't working so I went out to the Oxxo to get my Diet Coke, it was parked there, I got a good look at it. If Ezequiel Barraza was in his daughter's bedroom maybe he heard him, then he went to Altata and later on he let himself be seen by Mariana Kelly at the building where she lives. That is how an alcoholic would act. Or a troublemaker who wants to get caught. Let's go get him.

He called Beatriz. How's your father? He's drinking, I told him he's losing it. Are you at home? Yes, but I'm about to go out, I can't stand it any more, he won't stop telling me to get an abortion and I'm not going to do it; as far as I'm concerned this baby changed my life. Take it easy, go to a café, have some papaya juice, and think about your child's future, and do me a favour, look on your cell phone to see if Ezequiel called me two nights before the day he died; maybe you were in the bathroom or something, I'll call you back in two minutes.

For the first time he saw the S.U.V. with tinted windows. Olive green Cherokee. Dirty. He got hold of Beatriz again and yes, Barraza had made the call when she was in the bathroom.

Abelardo Rodríguez was drunk and by himself in the living room of his home. Detective Mendieta, how are you, come in both of you, he was listening to Rocío Dúrcal's "Amor eterno". What a delight to have you here, would you like a drink? It would be a pleasure. At last we'll have a drink with real glasses, which is only proper. Zelda gave her partner a puzzled look. And you, señorita? No, thank you, it's rather early for me. You're right, Paola used to say that avoiding alcohol is the best way to keep your skin looking fresh, although she didn't hold herself to that very often, my daughter was a volcano, you have no idea how much we miss her. He turned off the stereo. He poured. Your health, they said. Someplace in the world it must be five o'clock, the host added, and he downed it all. In an instant the tension rose. Will you have another, detective? he filled his own glass. I'd rather you tell us why you killed Ezequiel Barraza. Rodríguez looked at his whisky, then at Mendieta; defenceless, he smiled: You are right, detective, you do belong to the band of the bad guys, then he looked serious, his eyes grew moist; it was a father's motives, detective, that bastard was sleeping with both my daughters in my own house, several times I spoke with him, I insisted he show some respect for my home, and every time he just mocked me, his behaviour was utterly gross, he drained his glass, he left me no option; Beatriz is pregnant, can you imagine a child from that fiend? no way could I hold myself back, the only thing that weighs on me is the sorrow I've caused his mother. What about Bruno Canizales? That one I did not kill. Did you go to his house? I went there that very night, I followed Paola, I knew she was going to him and I got there ahead of her; I saw her go into the lawyer's home, I saw her come out. So Paola killed him. No, the time she was in there went by without a sound and my pistol does not have a silencer. What time was that? About six, the sun was about to come up; I had already showered to get ready for work when I heard her come home about 5.20, I heard her leave again and I followed her to Guadalupe. When you decided to sentence Ezequiel, did a call he made two nights before have anything to do with it? I know nothing about that. Why did you want to kill Mariana Kelly? I like you, detective, you guess everything. Why did you follow her all the way to Altata? She and Samantha Valdés threatened my daughter; I happened to run into them getting gas at Del Valle and saw them happy as could be, I don't know, it didn't seem fair that my daughter was dead and they were enjoying themselves as if nothing had happened; I followed them, I found where they stay on the beach and I went back two days later; the moment I pulled the trigger my foot sank into the sand and unfortunately I missed, the poor dog. But that wasn't enough, you turned up at her apartment. Well, yeah, I wanted to finish the job. And then you broke into her apartment at night. I broke into her apartment, you say? Yes, and you fired. No, that wasn't me, on Sunday I spied on them, that I won't deny, but I never tried to enter her house. The dog identified you. I don't doubt

215

it, they are very sensitive animals. Lefty remembered that Luigi kept wagging his tail when they chased the intruder down the stairs, who could it have been? And what about the silver bullets? They were a gift from Don Federico Villegas, may he rest in peace, about ten years ago we did some repairs to his country house and he gave me five; since they used silver bullets on Canizales I figured I would do the same, I thought it would put you off the trail. Who told you that Mariana Kelly and Samantha Valdés threatened your daughter? I read it in her diary, it has so many personal things I didn't dare give it to you; now there is no point in keeping it hidden, I have it in my desk, he pointed to the open door of the office, he stood up, and I'm pleased you're one of the bad guys even if all we ever talk about is this mess. The detective also stood up: I ought to go with you. I don't mind, by the way, your friend is a real looker, I saw her in Navolato when they all came out of the clinic and then again on the highway, he smiled. Mendieta held himself in check.

It was an office full of blueprints, with a bookcase crammed with folders and a big desk holding a computer and a collection of baseball caps, Rodríguez seemed relaxed, he sat down at the desk, he had let a weight slide off his shoulders. I've got it right here, he repeated, and he stuck his hand in a drawer, pulled out a pistol, and shot himself in the temple.

Mendieta contemplated his expression, then the pistol. Loyal to Pietro Beretta, he mumbled, we are nothing but a race of fucking romantics.

Forty-Four

They waited for Beatriz, gave her a version of the story that would allow her to come to terms with it, and they left the house. When they were pulling out, Dante arrived in his car, looking very serious. This kid is going places, the detective commented, he knows how to fit reality into a handful of symbols. His mother, utterly undone, was in the passenger seat.

At a crossroads where an officer was directing traffic, Zelda Toledo broke the silence: It is unbelievable how a family can destroy itself. Mendieta, who was thinking about Goga, answered: And Canizales' killer is still on the loose. Maybe he heard the case is closed and is living in peace. As far as I'm concerned he can rot in hell, they got the nod, the traffic cop waved to Zelda, to be frank I've just lost interest, I'm fed up with navigating around untouchables who break the law whenever they feel like it. There was a long pause. I'm just going on inertia, Zelda, besides, we've run out of suspects. What about Laura, Dania, the rest of the U.S.B. people? If it was one of them and we arrest them, they'll turn all the prisoners into vegetarians, imagine that, we'd better let things lie.

Cavalry charge. The detective saw it was Briseño. They were passing by the monument to Zapata on the way to Headquarters. The chef-in-chief, they smiled, what dish do you suppose they're cooking up? why doesn't he send her to cooking school so they can stop fighting? it can't be healthy to argue so much over a lentil soup. Mendieta. Lefty, I just found out that Pineda wouldn't let you take today's gangsta-wrap, just your luck, I've told you before, you always manage an easy landing. Thank you, chief. Listen, I need your discreet negotiating skills, that friend of yours from "Eyes on the Night" won't stop pestering, I'm sick and tired of him, he's got a campaign on about Canizales without naming him that comes out of nowhere, I want you to take care of that. Understood, have you got an envelope somewhere you don't know what to do with? What, do you think I work in Narcotics? In this country all the police work in Narcotics. Can you rein him in, I mean, enough so he doesn't keep shooting off his mouth? Chief, you told me to take care of it.

At Headquarters everything was the same. Angelita greeted them with a smile and a stack of messages. Honey, get us vouchers for gas. I already tried, they told me there's none until next month, they said to put water in it. Listen to that, what bastards.

Briseño told them it might be something orchestrated by his enemies. Those slimebags won't leave me alone, since when are they interested in Canizales and silver bullets? they're only going to incite the murderer to kill another innocent victim.

In his office he tried to stop thinking about Goga, whose calls he did not dare take, or about Bruno, who seemed linked to everything that came into his head anyway. Among the messages was one from L.H., he called: Friend, his colleague greeted him, I am partaking of a salmon with fine herbs, washed down with a Casa de Piedra merlot vintage '93. Me, I'm looking at a grilled mahi-mahi with nopal sauce, some roasted jalapeños, and an ice-cold Pacífico, what's up, my man L.H.? that's full of Omega-3, isn't it? Full of life itself, my man L.M., listen I called to say hello and to tell you that the fragrance you sent me is an Indian essential oil, it's called "So you won't forget me", and it's curious because, do you remember that I had to analyse a sample from San Bernadino? well, it turned out very similar to yours, if they weren't so far apart we might think the criminal is one and the same. Do you know anything about the victims? Not much: adult single men. Bisexuals? No idea, though a substantial portion of North Americans are. Silver bullets? I think so. Lefty began to sweat. Fucking case, it does not want to leave me, he pondered and said: Is there any known reason why people use that fragrance? No, not that I know of, it seems these are the first cases where it turned up; Indians associate it with wild sex, according to the myth, the cruel demon Ravana kidnaps Rama's consort Sita and hides her on an island, then Rama allies himself with a tribe of monkeys and rescues her, after which Sugriva, the leader of the monkeys, gives him the perfume so that on the night they reunite Sita will forget the suffering of her captivity and her submission will be complete; it's a lovely story of Eros without Thanatos, and according to Magda who did the research the bit about Thanatos only got added in when the fragrance arrived in the West, and the legend came to imply dying during the sexual act. But not from a bullet to the head, right? Listen, you're questioning me as if they hadn't closed the case. It's my goddamn professional deformation, L., what can you do; by the way did they mention any sect involved in the crimes? No, not that I know of, do you want me to find out? Don't bother, there's no reason, but if you hear of anything let me know. O.K., enjoy your fish. Thanks, I'll be seeing you.

What times we live in, my God, murderers who launch a craze: the profile of the victim, the silver bullets, the Indian fragrance, is this how it's always going to be? I'm so glad we aren't pursuing it.

Cavalry charge. Mendieta. Lefty, are you coming to eat? Trudis, why do you ask, I never go home for lunch, did you find a way to pay for the telephone bill? Oh, Lefty, where do you expect me to find that if you are my only support. Ask Walter Machado. I only asked him about romance and that sort of thing, you pay it, don't be bad, carve the debt in ice. You are shameless. But you are a nice guy. O.K., but this is going to be the last time. Listen, since I know you like it so much, I made a roast, come right now, what can you lose? if some delinquent gets away from you you'll catch him later. Leave it in the micro for me. Alright, just don't forget to add the vegetables; oh yes, a gringo called you. Enrique? No, I know your brother's voice, it was one I could barely understand, I think it's some relative of yours, his first name didn't stick, but his last name is Mendieta, just like you. Did he leave his number? No. If he calls again, ask him for it and give him my cell phone number. Lefty, can you believe it, Chespirito gave Lourdes a job, what did I tell you? as soon as he saw her he recognised her, you see blood doesn't lie, and that got Marco Antonio all excited and now he wants to find his father, so we did some digging, he's in Los Angeles, he's going to sing at the Kodak Theatre. You didn't make another long distance call, did you? Of course not, aren't you the suspicious one, Marcos made it from his school, pretty soon they'll be calling me in for his bad behaviour, but who cares, my poor son, he's desperate.

Text number twenty-six from Goga arrived. Fucking she-devil, no way am I going to open this, he looked at the screen and felt stupid. Why not? What could happen to me that hasn't already? He felt his blood run cold, hot. All in all, another stripe on the tiger.

He opened it: "idiot, brute, cretin, stuck-up, neurotic, coward, hope u die". Yikes, he furrowed his brow, now let the bitch talk about maturity.

At that moment he wanted to go far away, would his savings be enough to buy him time on another planet while he looked for work? He could teach literature in a high school or proofread at a newspaper. Go. Vanish. Get lost. Can a man change his life? Zelda came in: Boss, it's snack time, shall we?

At El Quijote, Curlygirl welcomed them with cold beers: Edgar, where have you been hiding? everyone keeps coming except you, I've marked you down as absent. Work, Curlygirl, you know. Ah, it's been busy here too, every day people are drunker and wilder, aren't they? At this rate we're all going to die of cirrhosis. Or of something worse, they smiled, Zelda, you look divine, my queen, where did you get your hair done? In my neighbourhood. They did a fabulous job, you look like Thalía at her best, have you never thought of colouring it like Shakira? it would suit you. Do you think so, wouldn't it be a little too flashy? So what, girlie, if you don't show off now, then when? He ran his fingers through it: You've kept it really healthy. I'll surprise you one of these days. Listen, Edgar, sweetie, put the brakes on the narco-juniors, nobody can stand them, they turn up, they have their awful fights, and they leave as if nothing happened, it is simply not fair. First we have to solve the problem of the narco-seniors, they've taken to killing each other and wrapping the bodies in blankets. They are all crazy, what would you like, my dear? The works. For me too, Curlygirl, and also let me have a roast pork sandwich to go. Right away.

They were served fish soup, fried porgy, and breaded shrimp. An hour later.

What shall we do? Scratch our bellies. Too boring, if you like we can visit Señora Villegas. What a drag. I'm just saying, it's something to do, we were headed there this morning. The case is closed, Zelda, and I've lived through so many emotions over the past few days that now I really want to think about something else; he signalled for the bill, Curlygirl brought it over. Edgar, do you remember those girls? one night you came they sat over there, a little faggot was with them, a tranny. You told me what family they were from. Well, somebody kidnapped one of them on Saturday. Who? They say it was Marcelo Valdés' people; you saw how outrageous they were, well, they were flirting with everybody when a blond guy they call the Gringo, he was sitting over there, stood up, grabbed her by the arm, and dragged her outside, the girl was screaming like a banshee, but who was going to defend her, not even Chapulín Colorado. Careful, he might turn up. Oh, apple of your mother's eye, what times those were when I got all the looks, now all I get is pity. Don't say that, you don't look your age, Zelda insisted. Thank you, my queen, the sandwich is on me. A former cheerleader for the Tomateros, right? It was the other one he carried off, a beautiful dark-skinned girl. Mendieta surged to his feet. What happened? Zelda swept the room with her eyes as she caressed her pistol, he pulled a bill from the envelope for Quiroz and gave it to the waiter: Keep the change. Isn't that too much? You deserve it.

They got into the Jetta. Boss, are you alright? Sure, however we are going to do a couple of things, we'll keep sclerosis at bay and it may turn out to be more interesting than visiting Señora Villegas.

He called Montaño, who answered on the five-hundredth ring: What's up. Where are you? Where I always am, it's lunchtime, can't you leave me in peace? I need a favour. Not now, Lefty, I'm busy. It's an easy one for you, the cheerleader for the Tomateros you sometimes go with has a tranny friend I'd like to talk to. No kidding, then it's true about the flowers in your office? What can I tell you, my luck with women is so awful that I lost my fear of turning queer. The midlife crisis hit hard, eh? hang on, he heard him whispering, she says she knows several, which one. Are you with her? You're a wizard! your timing couldn't have been better. The one that went with her to El Quijote a week ago. Wait, she's getting her book; can I tell you something, Mendieta? you have no idea how beautiful she looks when she walks naked, she's from another world: graceful, splendiferous, voluptuous, he sighed, incredibly erotic, an insuperable vision of loveliness; here she comes . . . his name is Alexis Valenzuela. He gave him the cell phone number.

He remained lost in thought. Not only cats, some people have nine lives and always land on their feet, they were still parked outside the restaurant. Sometimes memory is a curse, he concluded. Zelda plainly did not understand: Boss, shall I call Valenzuela? Find out if he can see us this afternoon. What about Señora Villegas? Let's forget her, we are onto something else and like I told you I don't want to hear any more about Canizales and even less about people who had nothing to do with it. But isn't Valenzuela part of it too? Trust me, Zelda Toledo, and don't be a pain; while we have nothing else to do we can follow up on a few details, the victim's social life, for example, remember, he used to dress up as a woman and, why not? something about silver bullets. He told her about Rendón's theory. As long as something interesting keeps turning up, let's keep it from Narcotics.

They crossed the Tamazula River on the Orabá Island bridge.

They turned right onto Valadés Parkway, since they had time for a little tour before their appointment. The traffic was intense. He braked suddenly in front of the building where Mariana lived. Three bodyguards were in view. Wait here. What am I doing? he hesitated, living out my stupidity, I wouldn't want to forget how, Goga's probably not here, and why didn't Luigi bark that night?

One of the bodyguards recognised him and went to meet him, he had been with the judicial police: Chief Mendieta, what a pleasure for the eyes. Devil Urquídez, my man, what's up, how are you? Never better, thanks to God and Most Holy Mary who always holds us in her hands, he kissed a gold medallion. You said it, so what are you doing here? A babe, girlfriend of the boss' daughter, she's afraid of some asshole and we're staking him out. Has he turned up? Do you think he would try it with us here? Not in this life, is anyone in the apartment? Nobody, yesterday they went to Don Marcelo's house; listen, you are never going to die, ever, on Saturday we were talking about you, my father-in-law is a big fan. Who is your father-in-law? Shorty Abitia, he says you've known each other since you were little kids. Are you going out with Begoña? We're engaged, if God grants it we'll tie the knot in November. Well, congratulations and please give my best to Shorty, isn't Begoña studying something? Yes, but once she's with me why would she want to go to school, neither she nor her family will ever lack for a thing, God willing. You are right, Devil my man, O.K., I'll see you later. You aren't going in? This isn't where I'm headed, see you. Cavalry charge. It was Briseño, but he let it ring.

They met Valenzuela at the bar in the Hotel Lucerna. The tranny's cell phone would not stop ringing and he would not stop answering it. He was a strong, wiry man of average height with a deep voice. Pardon us bothering you. It's nothing, if Keiko says I should talk to you, I will talk to you, how could I not? cell phone again. Hello handsome, aha, look for him at the Arts Council, sweetheart, of course, could you hang on a moment? the conversation I am in the middle of can't be postponed, I'll call you in a little while. Do you mind if we speak without interruptions? it won't take long. Go right ahead, he put it on vibrate; I am all yours, commander, listen you look really relaxed, I can see you like your work. Zelda spoke up: Did you know Attorney Bruno Canizales? Oh, the poor man, I heard, he was at a party with us months ago, Isadora brought him. Who? Francisco Aldana, the modern dancer you people saw in Mazatlán, by the way he is terrified, he didn't do anything, did he? Until we catch the culprit we can't be sure, Zelda slipped in. Canizales was rather, shall we say, informal in his love life, rumour had it he'd taken to cruising, he would go to Guamúchil or some other city not too far away; that can be incredibly exciting, but it is rather dangerous. Do you know anyone he picked up? We barely knew him and from what Frank told me he was not a lover to be trusted, he even went after Loca Adams, apparently they too had an affair; you understand, the drama of bisexuals; the truth is, I doubt Frank would have committed the crime, he's fragile and impressionable, insecure. Canizales was killed with a silver bullet, have you heard of

225

anyone using them? Commander, why would you ask that, do I look like a crook? I'm for world peace, mind you the day you saw me with Keiko we had come from the cemetery, it was the anniversary of the murder of a boyfriend of mine, I went to pieces, and I think it was with a silver bullet, those were such sad times I can't remember most of it. What was his name? Klaus Timmerman, a big white guy, well hung, my God how I miss him, and you know he wasn't young, about forty, but he sizzled like nobody since. Was there an investigation? Oh yes, I spoke several times with a policeman, he thought I killed him, the same way you accused Isadora, oh no, my poor Klaus. Did they tell you who the culprit was? You know how it is, maybe they told his family, who by the way despised me, and I was in such a bad way I never asked. Have you heard of anyone else knocked off with a silver bullet? Captain, sadness clouds my thinking, have you never lost a love? Does Klaus' family live here? All of them: wife, children, parents, siblings. O.K., we hope not to bother you any more. It's no problem, commander, whenever you like, and please find the culprit because if you don't, who knows what will become of poor Isadora. Here, write Klaus' address down on this.

In the hotel parking lot he called Ortega. I'm so glad you called. Spill it or I won't give you your lunch money. Last night they found a bright red car in the Rosales Canal and inside was a new model Smith & Wesson, I'll test it to see if it's the weapon we're looking for. Did they find any papers? Nothing, the car was a gypsy, yet another, as if the traffic weren't atrocious enough, neither did we find any prints. Hey, don't you know the case is closed? No kidding, and here I am stuck on it. So it hasn't ended for you either. When a case isn't over there's a certain inertia, we exist inside it; is there news,

Lefty? since you didn't call just to say hello, I know you inside out. A year ago Klaus Timmerman Acevedo got killed, probably with a silver bullet, do you remember that? A year ago I spent three weeks in Vancouver taking a macramé course, what about you? I was taking crochet in Tijuana. That was when it all happened with the girl, right? He ignored that, but recalled that it had happened three months later. If they assigned it to us, Sánchez must know something, I'll have to visit him in the country. Leave him alone, I'll look in the archives, a year ago you say? A year ago last week. I'll call you in a little while, listen, thanks for helping Memo, he got a ten on the exam and he's even reading *The Burning Plain*, he says with that novel he'll have read the complete works of Rulfo. He told you it was a novel? No, why? They're short stories. Isn't that the same thing? You aren't any stupider because you aren't any older. Go fuck a duck. What's the name of those rare butterflies you found on Canizales' car? Guasachiatas. See you. He hung up.

Ernestina de Villegas greeted them effusively, offered them coffee, and told them the story of the silver bullets left by her late husband. For a long time they sat in a glass case in the country, until my son René took them from the new addition that indeed Señor Abelardo Rodríguez built for us, poor man, I heard that a daughter of his committed suicide. Did your husband like to shoot silver bullets? Never, he kept them to show off to his friends and at Christmas he would give them as gifts, he bought bullets of different brands and calibres. Then your son shot them. Why would you think that, he's a gentle soul, he must have them at his house and for sure he does the same as Federico, may God hold him in his holy glory. Where could

227

I find him? Right here, he lives in Los Angeles but he came to bring me back and to pick up his wife; he must be at his house in Guadalupe, he lives on Río Presidio, would you like me to call him? No, señora, we have no reason to bother him. You can see him in that picture from his wedding, the biggest one, next to ours. Mendieta glanced at the family photo gallery, but showed no interest. Someone was killed with a silver bullet, my compadre Carlos told me. Two, señora. God Almighty, I hope they catch the murderer, what a mess we're in with all these gangsta-wraps. Alright, Señora Villegas, thank you for the information. In reality he felt exasperated, the case was closed and they were wasting their time; he had done it for Zelda, who he could see was really antsy, however, he reminded himself, he should not be making this sort of concession, what was he playing at? They stood up, he was at the end of his rope and Parra had taught him to recognise that feeling of helplessness and to control it, so would it not be better to take a tranquiliser and go back to reading *News from the Empire*? by now he was totally caught up in the book. Whatever I can do for you, señores, I am pleased to be of service. On the way out he paused a long moment before the photograph of René and his wife: two long-haired young people, smiling, ready to take on the world.

Before he was out the door, his cell phone rang.

There you are, Ortega exclaimed, Timmerman was killed with a silver bullet and to make you even more happy with a Smith & Wesson, one year ago, they found him in the living room of his house with a bullet in the head. Did he live alone? At the time his family was on vacation in Germany. Was Sánchez in charge? No, it was Ernesto Ponce's last case, your great friend the Gringo. Do you

228

believe it was the same pistol they used to kill Canizales? It's the same type, the models don't change much, are you still stuck on that, my child? Is there any record of the investigation or detainees? They interrogated his family, two brothers, father and mother, three neighbours, and four times Alexis Valenzuela, with whom he had a romantic relationship, according to what's in here, and also René Villegas, a friend of the victim. He hung up.

He was seized by a sudden feeling of dread, and pulled the car over. They were on Valadés Parkway beside the Chapultepec Golf Club. He got out and walked the pavement, unable to speak. He stopped. He took a step. He stopped again. Zelda, at a prudent distance, understood that something inside him was falling to pieces.

For three minutes he remained in that state. At last he took a long look up at the sky and went over to his partner: Agent Toledo, do you believe in the power of hugs? She muttered, yes. Well, give me your biggest because I'm going to hell in a handbasket.

Forty-Five

The only good cop is a dead cop, he declared once they were under way again, if the Mexican police were honest I wouldn't make the grade. They fell silent until they had René Villegas' house in sight, a residence the detective had seen many times before. Muted lighting. Garden. Garage. An almond tree by the curb. Inside the garage, a midsize sedan. Zelda was all wound up, she wanted to know but could not bring herself to ask, who was Loca Adams?

I am going to begin with the flowers, the detective said at last without taking his eyes off the two-storey home. He told her about meeting up with Goga, the backstory, their recent time together, and the husband's telephone call. He finished with the text message, which he showed her, Zelda read it and remained silent, she was trying to put it all together without asking questions. So, who killed Bruno Canizales? I don't know and the truth is I don't care. And so it was: his intuition was telling him he was facing a menace that had more to do with him than anything else; there was the business of the silver bullets and the murder of Timmerman, but that was not enough. He was not certain of anything and that was what hit hardest: appreciating his own insignificance when faced with the impossible. He did not feel like explaining it. He could not anyway, he did not know how. Nothing is true, nothing is false. What he hoped, now that the moment had arrived, was that her spatial intelligence would help his feet find the ground. They live in the States, he mumbled. What does that mean? Did you see

René's wedding picture? I took a quick look. The bride is Goga.

During the next three minutes neither one of them said a thing. Who is Loca Adams? No idea.

Mendieta thought about "Hamlet", about maybe having a seventeen-year-old son, about how hard it is to love, even Bardominos came to mind. In reality love is the search for an other who does not exist, yet has cunningly polluted our identity.

The cell phone beeped an incoming message. It was from Goga. He glanced down and handed it to Zelda: Open it. Zelda read it and gave it back: Better if you read it. "Forgive me, luv u, want to c u." Mendieta was again plunged into himself. What sort of person have I been in love with? could this be a trap? are they watching? Goga Fox: you do not exist, I never knew you, never made love to you, never saw you walk to the bathroom. He turned to his partner: Zelda. Shall I call for reinforcements? No, you'll have to let me go in alone, as you can tell, this is personal and I wouldn't want anything to happen to you. Boss, I'm your partner. I know, but this is so complicated that it'd be better for you not to get involved. Don't do this to me, if I stay here I'll go crazy, I swear; if I get the feeling I shouldn't be there, I'll take off, I promise. He took his pistol out of the glove compartment, she took hers out of her bag, they opened the doors. May it be as God wishes.

Knock, knock, knock.

They could hear soft music. Villegas opened the door. Waft of a familiar scent. Mendieta recalled him from the only time he had seen him in Altata the first time he met Goga, and also from a few days ago when he visited the Canizales compound: he was the man with the girls and the brother. His attire was neat and stylish. René

231

Villegas, we are from the police, hands up, you are accused of the murders of Bruno Canizales, Klaus Timmerman, and at least two more in San Bernadino, California. René smiled, he had what looked like a rum and coke in his hand, Zelda Toledo had her gun trained on him. How are you planning to prove that, you scum? Yes, how do you plan to prove it? mocked Goga, coming into view behind her husband wearing her loose skirt, her flowered blouse, and a sarcastic smile. The Mexican police are nothing but shit, a bunch of idiots, rotten and corrupt, Villegas added without losing his ironic tone. Mendieta smacked him across the head three times and gave him a kick in the groin. That's how, asshole, our infallible method. Don't hit him, shrieked Goga, furious and threatening Mendieta with her nails. You won't even be able take me in, continued the husband, catching his breath, blood was trickling from one ear, my friends won't let that happen, and believe me I've got them all the way to the top, besides you don't have any proof; you know what you've got in your head? shit; he took a swig from a bottle of rum he had at hand, you stupid son of a bitch. And who told you we need any proof to bust your ass, eh? he kicked him again and smacked him on the neck. Zelda kept her gun on the couple, who ignored her, Villegas reeled, Goga stepped between them: Leave him alone, you Neanderthal. You, get over there, he shoved her hard, a lamp and several porcelain knick-knacks tumbled, didn't you want to see me, Loca Adams? Her face fell. I like that nickname, it sends me, it incites me, Zelda took her by the arm, Goga pushed her away: Let go, you bitch, she looked at Mendieta, her eyes out of orbit, I was dying to see you, don't you feel it? don't my pheromones excite you? and look, imbecile, apart from your brutality you have nothing on René, what is all this about him killing Klaus Timmerman? admit it, your rival is much smarter than you, more astute, better looking, and he has you beaten, she was livid and Villegas was smiling, the rum spilling out of the bottle. It's true, I don't know if it was you or him that murdered Canizales. Don't make me laugh, how are you going to prove that? By your Indian perfume, "So you won't forget me". Goga stopped smiling, it was the fragrance she was giving off at that very moment, the same one the detective smelled when he opened the door. You dolt, she howled and she leapt at him, but Zelda, who thought in images, did crossword puzzles, and played chess with Rodo, laid her out cleanly, handcuffed her, and then cuffed the husband, who was weaving, a bit seasick. You still won't find anything to pin on us, you idiot, you won't get me to confess, it's your word against mine. Zelda, call Ortega, tell him to bring the sweeper. Then he called Gori Hortigosa, the specialist in problematic confessions. My man Gori, how's the fuse. I'm fine, my man Lefty, here celebrating my daughter's fifteenth birthday. Could you do a job? Is it urgent? More or less. You know it is my vocation. I'll meet you at the Cathedral in an hour. He turned to Villegas: In the Cathedral everyone confesses, to date no-one has kept any secrets from Gori Hortigosa, you decide. The husband smiled: We beat you, Lefty Mendieta, admit it. Goga glared at him unblinking: You are a second-rate detective and a novice in bed. She had had enough of you, the husband added, a guy who doesn't know how to make love, doesn't know how to do anything, after Canizales you were her worst student. Is that why you waited for him that Thursday to kill him? That's why and because he didn't want to dress up as a girl, he claimed he didn't have the clothes with him, he also resisted something else which he considered a humiliation, something you submitted to like a lamb, we didn't even need our perfume's narcotic spell, except that today you were fated to die, are you recording this? because I don't care. Mendieta held in check his urge to crush him. We killed him together, Goga said proudly. Of course, sweetheart, although I arranged the sheets myself I am not blaming you, and nothing is going to happen to us, in a couple of hours we'll get out of this and we'll go far away, on the other side we'll find someone to play with; well, perhaps we'll leave a souvenir for that guy Quiroz, who has been an utter pain in the ass; the other night you only escaped by a miracle. Forgive me for falling asleep, Goga said with a smile, and this idiot believed you were calling from the airport.

How long did you wait for Canizales? Three hours, the asshole had gone to Mazatlán to see Isadora. At first we had other plans, to have a good time and all, but he took so long and waiting is always aggravating. He remembered the kid with the bike. We have a witness who saw you coming out. It doesn't matter, you can't beat us, we have enough money to buy the Supreme Court if we need to. Not even his call at Christmas was enough for you to forgive him. Forgiveness is for weaklings and retards, not us. What about the Smith & Wesson? It's in my closet with the bullets I have left, we satisfied Bruno's wish, right, my love? Goga did not answer.

A car pulled up.

The detectives thought it was Guillermo Ortega, but no, it was Samantha Valdés and Mariana Kelly. Oh no, Mendieta, you again? sheesh, don't you ever get tired of bothering me? now what? Mariana understood immediately, she grabbed Samantha by the arm: I think we should leave right now, Sam, please, I'm begging you. They killed Bruno Canizales, the detective said. Samantha's jaw dropped. Is it true? her eyes were blazing. Fuck. It was a lamentable accident, Sam, that's all. Were you involved with him? Not at all, why get excited? you didn't love him either, Goga pointed out scornfully. Mariana pulled her towards the door: Sam, please, for me. What a shitty thing to do, fucking Goga, I didn't love him, but my son did. Don't be ridiculous, the husband intervened, stop talking crap and call your muscle so this Neanderthal will leave us alone. You are mistaken, you fucking slummy faggot, you must have shit for brains if you think I'm going to let this lie, she was trembling with rage; I suspected you had something to do with Bruno, but I didn't believe you had it in you. Don't exaggerate, it's no big deal. Samantha pressed her lips together: You don't say, would you like to tell me what is important? you must live on the fucking moon; Mendieta, do me a favour, I don't like you one bit, that you know, but in good faith leave them to me, the case is closed, you said so yourself, and if Bruno's death pains my son then it pains me too, shit, also because of all the things I told you about; let the water flow, Mendieta, let the fur fly. Mariana stiffened. Zelda fixed her with a glare.

Goga was the first to change her tune: Don't do it, Edgar, do your duty and let the courts try us, the twenty or thirty years they give us we'll manage to get through somehow. I think that would be best, the husband echoed her, listen, all the stuff I said I was just kidding, you really are a wonderful policeman, would you like to know about the silver bullets? besides the fact that he wanted it, contrary to Timmerman, it was a game. Samantha slapped him: Shut up, asshole, you and your little games, she turned to the detective, so? Hang on a minute, how many more did you kill in San Bernadino?

Mendieta, don't get pushy, buddy, besides what good would it do you?

Take off their handcuffs, he ordered his partner. Edgar, I beg you, I truly did want to see you, make love to you, talk to you, do that little sashay, don't you see how I'm dressed? Zelda, deeply upset, went ahead. Samantha called her bodyguards, Goga continued begging for forgiveness, two unfamiliar faces came in, they looked sunburned, one was carrying an A.K. I'll get the blankets, the other grumbled as he climbed the stairs to the second floor where the bedroom had to be, the one with the rifle covered their mouths with packing tape and tied their hands behind them.

They left.

While he was calling Ortega he watched them take the couple out and put them in the bodyguards' black Hummer. Where are you? Close by, at Obregón and Zapata. Forget it, there's nothing. Lefty, what happened? Jack the Ripper, he did it again. Aha, and you couldn't find any better entertainment than to call me? Right, but I don't want any trouble with Sarita. Shall I confess something? in reality I couldn't go, Pineda asked for a hand in Piggyback, who do you think got whacked? No idea. Your friend the Gringo, along with a girl and two triggermen. Well, let's hope he makes good use of you, see you later. He hung up. He watched the women get into the green Hummer and pull out, the black one close behind, heading towards the Coast Highway. At that moment he was telling Gori Hortigosa to stay home with his guests.

Boss, Zelda gave him back his handcuffs, did we do the right thing? I doubt it, shall we go? They got into the Jetta.

*

The following day the city was shaken by the notoriety and beauty of the gangsta-wraps, as well as by the savagery with which they had been massacred. There were statements from their friends, promises by the authorities to end the violence, and a march demanding that the crime be solved. "Eyes on the Night" doubled its rating and its star reporter became a serious candidate for journalist of the year. Gringo Ponce and the rest did not merit a mention.

As soon as he was alone, Mendieta broke down and wept. He did not want to, but nothing convinced him otherwise. He cursed life, love, and short-haired women. He cursed himself. On Dr Parra's advice, he spent a few days in Mazatlán, where he met a brown-skinned woman who had one green eye and the other the colour of honey; she was also a lefty, but that is another tale.

ÉLMER MENDOZA was born in Culiacán, México in 1949. He is a professor and author, widely regarded as the founder of "narco-lit", which explores drug trafficking and corruption in Latin America. He won the José Fuentes Mares National Literary Prize for *Janis Joplin's Lover*, and the Tusquets Prize for *Silver Bullets*.

MARK FRIED is a literary translator specialising in Latin American literature. He lives in Ottawa, Canada.